THE WALL PEOPLE
(In Search of a Home)

THE WALL PEOPLE

(In Search of a Home)

By **Joseph J. Di Certo**

Illustrated by Frederic Marvin

Atheneum   1985   New York

Library of Congress Cataloging in Publication Data

Di Certo, Joseph.
The wall people.

SUMMARY: The Calabashes, a family of five-inch people
who live between the walls and ceilings of New York
apartment buildings, move to a new home, and discover new danger.
1. Children's stories, American. [1. Fairies—
Fiction. 2. New York (N.Y.)—Fiction. 3. Apartment
houses—Fiction. 4. Moving, Household—Fiction.
5. Burglary—Fiction] I. Title.
PZ7.D5416Wal 1985 [Fic] 84-21535
ISBN 0-689-31090-0

Published simultaneously in Canada by
McClelland & Stewart, Ltd.
Composition by Maryland Linotype,
Baltimore, Maryland
Printed and bound by Fairfield Graphics,
Fairfield, Pennsylvania
Designed by Marilyn Marcus
First Edition

*In honor of my mother and father,
who never stopped believing in me
and died with a great dream
still in their hearts.*

Contents

THE WALL PEOPLE

(In Search of a Home)

1 ✳ A Bad Start

Zort W. Calabash leaned against the mantel clock and surveyed the elegant living room with its twenty-foot-high ceiling and handsomely paneled walls. It was tastefully furnished and beautifully decorated for the Christmas season. Zort's long, thin face crinkled into a smile. *Yes, this will do fine*, he thought. He was the tallest of the Calabash Clan, standing a full five inches (although he insisted he was five and a quarter), and had

3

thick, bushy eyebrows, which perched like awnings above his emerald green eyes. His graying, light brown hair suggested that Zort had entered the autumn of his years. He claimed to be only ninety-five, though it was common knowledge that he had long since passed his one hundred and twenty-fifth birthday. But there was no questioning Zort's dress habits . . . formal. He dressed formally at all times—white tie and tails, top hat and spats—whether working, playing or relaxing. His dress was the thing that made him different.

Excited by the idea of living in such an elegant house, Zort leaped before he looked, landing on the thick living room carpet. For a few seconds he studied his surroundings, unaware that he was being watched, until a terrifying creature came racing across the room.

Zort, awakened to his danger, leaped like a coiled spring to a nearby table. Then there was a tense moment of silence. He stared down to see the beast crouched and ready to burst upon him for the final kill. Instantly Zort closed his eyes and squeezed his face in an act of super concentration. The moment the creature sprang, a large chair slid in the way, sending him crashing to the floor.

"You nearly killed me. 'Tis a brute you are," said Zort crossly, picking up his top hat and smoothing down his hair. "For a house cat, you are awfully ferocious."

The cat, who was brown and gray with black and white stripes, very fat and terribly crossed-eyed, sat up and blinked a few times, trying hard to steady himself and ignore the painful bump on his head. "Feels more like you nearly killed me. How'd you do that?"

"To be sure, how I did it is my concern and not to be known by the likes of you. Staying alive is also my concern, so let's not try any more of your antics or you'll end up with a lot worse than a bump on your head," Zort answered sharply. "What's your name?"

The fat feline hesitated.

"What's wrong?" asked Zort impatiently. "Don't you have a name?"

The cat lowered his head. "Sure I do. It's just that . . . well . . ." Then he looked up pleadingly. "You won't laugh, will you?"

"Certainly not," assured Zort. "A name is nothing to laugh at."

"All right. My name . . . ah." He hesitated again. "My name is . . . ah . . . Rhinoceros," he finally blurted out.

"Rhinoceros?" asked Zort, to be sure he had heard correctly. "Rhinoceros, is it?"

"Rhinoceros," repeated the cat timidly, drooping his furry head nearly down to the floor.

Zort's mouth spread to a smile, then to a broad grin: finally he broke into uncontrollable laughter.

Rhinoceros looked indignant. "You said you wouldn't laugh. I knew I shouldn't have told you."

Zort could barely talk. "I'm really . . . ho-ho, ha-ha . . . sorry. I just couldn't . . . he-he, ho-ho . . . help it. How could anyone tag you with such a name?"

"You don't know Di Napoli children."

"The who?" asked Zort.

"Julie and Joey Di Napoli. They live here with their parents and Nonno, Mrs. Di Napoli's father."

"Well, never mind about your name. 'Tis as good as any, I suppose, and no worse than some I've heard. It's not what anyone gets out of it, it's what you put into your name that counts." Zort cleared his throat. "Now, I suggest we be friends. It'll be easier on both of us."

"Sounds okay to me. But I don't know your name or where you live."

"The name, sir, is Calabash, Zort W. Calabash. As for our abode, from tonight on, we may possibly be living here."

"We? Who's we?" asked Rhinoceros, cocking his furry head to one side.

"We, my dear fellow, are myself, my nephew, his wife and four children, and my mother, a veritable fortress of a woman."

"How ya all gonna live in this apartment without being seen?"

"Oh, we've been doing this sort of thing for years. We live in the walls or, more correctly, in the space between the ceilings and the floors, and we only come out late at night."

Rhinoceros' eyes got wide and his whiskers twitched, as though he wanted to make sure he wasn't dreaming.

"Wow! Wall People living here. Are there many others?"

"Our family is part of a huge clan of people who live in buildings all along Park Avenue. There are twenty families living in this building alone. There are the O'Tooles on the seventh floor, the Ferriters on the ninth, and the O'Moores with their ten children on the third floor. Faith, there are over three hundred families in other buildings along Park Avenue."

"Are there any in that new building across the street?" Rhinoceros asked.

"No one lives there," Zort answered in a rather sharp voice. "We can't live in the new buildings. They're made of solid concrete . . . no spaces between the floors."

"Gee, that's too bad. The new buildings sort

of threaten you, don't they?" the cross-eyed cat said sympathetically.

"That they do, that they do. Things are changing," said Zort. "It used to be so wonderful along Park Avenue when I was young." His voice became soft, and he spoke as though he were looking at a beautiful vision that had suddenly appeared before him.

" 'Twas very close to being a bit of paradise, you might say. Here we were in the middle of a great city, on an elegant street lined with great mansions. Yet it was also like being in the country, though free of wild beasts. Many of the blocks were still undeveloped. Trees, tall grass and bushes abounded. It was quiet and unthreatening at night and in the early hours of the morning." He looked at Rhinoceros with practically a pleading expression. "We could almost live like normal human beings."

Neither of them spoke for a moment. Then Zort remembered that he still had a lot to do and was annoyed with himself for becoming sentimental. "You will have to excuse me now, Rhinoceros; I must be about my business. Will you be so kind as to direct me to the kitchen?"

"Sure. That's my favorite place. Go through the dining room. It's to your left. Just watch out for Mountain."

"Mountain?" What or who is Mountain?" asked Zort curiously.

"Oh, you'll find out soon enough," answered Rhinoceros with a smirk as he ambled off. Zort watched the plump furball waddle away. He tipped his hat, straightened his bow tie and gracefully jumped to the floor. The mantel clock announced 1:00 a.m. Zort walked to a corner of the room, picked up his bag of tools and headed for the kitchen.

At the entrance to the dining room, he peeked in to make sure all was clear. The room was a showcase of elegance: a large, highly polished table surrounded by ten handsomely carved chairs; an antique sideboard, upon which sat silver candlesticks, serving bowls, trays and a coffee holder. Zort was busy being impressed when suddenly he felt something fall upon him, like a giant marshmallow, only heavier. It crushed him to the floor. He could barely breathe under its weight. It didn't require super intelligence to realize that he had just encountered Mountain.

Zort nearly panicked, but quickly regained his self-control. He reached into his bag, grabbed a sharp tool and jabbed his attacker. With a yelp and a growl, the weight eased from him. Zort rolled free and sprang to his feet. Before him was a St. Bernard, its huge shaggy head resting on the floor between his two oversized paws, one of which had been resting on Zort.

"That was terribly inconsiderate. Lord knows, I could have suffocated," said Zort.

The dog was overwhelmed. His soft brown eyes blinked, and he cocked his head first to one side then to the other. "You're talking! You're talking my language!"

"Certainly I am. Communicating with most creatures, human or otherwise, is just one of my talents. You, sir, I presume are Mountain?"

"Right! Hey! You know a lot for such a little fellow. How come you're so small? Are you a fairy? Or an elf? Can you do magic?" Mountain asked excitedly.

Zort reacted sharply. He stood very straight and pressed his long, bony forefinger against Mountain's soft wet nose. "Let's get one thing straight this instant. I, Zort W. Calabash, and my clan are not—and I repeat, are not—fairies or elves, neither are we brownies, gnomes, nixies, goblins, trolls, dwarfs, pixies, kobalds, banshees, sylphs, sprites or undines. We do not, and never have, cast spells or bewitched people. Nor do we cause the sudden death of cattle. We are as human as any human that has ever walked the earth. Is that perfectly clear?"

"Gee, I didn't mean anything bad. Honest! It's just that you're so little and so old looking."

"Size is relative," snapped Zort. "Next to a whale you're tiny. Regarding my age, I'm only ninety-five . . . well . . . maybe a few years older."

"Ninety-five! It must be great to live that many years," said Mountain.

"In time you will learn that it's not how many years you use up, it's how you use the years that matters" counseled Zort.

They spoke for a few minutes, Zort having to explain that he and his family were forced to move from their home on 89th Street because the building was being torn down so that a new high-rise could be built.

"I guess you're sad about having to leave your home," said Mountain.

"Mountain, you can't imagine how heart-breaking it is. We had been living in that building for seventy-two years. My nephew was born there. He married there and brought four beautiful children into the world." He paused, deep in thought, murmuring softly to himself, "So many memories, so many memories." Then he looked at Mountain. "But that's all behind us now . . . progress is overtaking our world. The problem is progress may end up killing us all. As I always say, one man's progress can be another man's prison."

"For a little man you're pretty smart, and kinda nice." Mountain suddenly rose, nuzzled his nose against Zort and gave him a juicy lick, the force of which sent the little man tumbling to the floor.

"Stop it! Or I'll give you another jab," protested Zort. "There's a time for play and a time for work. Right now I have work to do."

"Can I help?" Mountain asked excitedly, his bushy tail wagging furiously.

"Yes," Zort answered curtly. "You can point out the entrance to the kitchen, then find a cozy corner and go to sleep."

Mountain looked disappointed. "It's at the end of the room, on the left. Be careful you don't fall over Hour Hand in the dark," he cautioned as he walked away.

"Who's—" Zort paused and decided not to ask. Obviously, the Di Napoli children had a veritable menagerie.

The interruptions put him behind schedule. There was much to be done. He had to survey the entire apartment, gathering all kinds of information that would help him to decide whether or not the family could live here with some sense of security. So far, the prospects didn't look too good. Animals were always a threat to the Wall People; they were awake at all hours of the night. Then there were the Di Napoli children. Zort had to think about all these factors and a lot more. He walked rapidly between the dining room table, on his right, and a large breakfront containing fine china and silverware, on his left. He was thinking about the food he would find in the kitchen as he made a fast left turn around the breakfront.

Wham! He crashed into what seemed to be

a large stone. *A large stone? In the dining room?* he thought as he flopped on his face, rolled to one side and landed on his back.

"Good lord and all the saints in heaven! Now what?" Zort moaned. He sprang to his feet, ready to fight, ready to jump, ready for anything. But nothing happened. The darkness was relieved only slightly by a few traces of light drifting through the richly draped window. It was enough for Zort to see that the object before him was indeed rocklike. Suddenly, two shiny eyes appeared and began to blink. Zort quickly concluded that this was Hour Hand, a box turtle.

"I . . . hope . . . you . . . didn't . . . hurt . . . yourself," said the turtle.

"Only my shinbone. I'm okay, considering I was also attacked by Rhinoceros and stepped on by Mountain. And before you ask, my name is Zort W. Calabash."

"I'm . . . Hour . . . Hand . . ." said the turtle.

" 'Tis an appropriate name to be sure."

"I . . . haven't . . . seen . . . you . . . around . . . here . . . before."

"If I survive this night, you may be seeing a lot of me from now on. I'm trying to decide whether or not our clan should move in.

"Ya . . . mean . . . you're going to live . . . with . . . the Di Napolis?"

"Sort of. We'll live in the walls, or to be precise, in the space between the ceiling of this apartment and the roof of the building. There's plenty of room there for even a large clan."

Hour Hand studied the small man for a few seconds. "You . . . sure . . . are . . . small . . . size . . . people. You are people, aren't you?"

Zort raised his eyebrows. "Certainly!" he answered indignantly. "We are human beings. A bit smaller, that's all. But it's not size that makes one human. If that were the case, some people would be a lot more human than others. We are human all right, 'tis just that our problems are a lot bigger than those of the big people.

"Are . . . there . . . many . . . of . . . you?" asked Hour Hand.

"Twenty other clans in this building, a couple of hundred clans living in other buildings along Park Avenue. We lived on Eighty-ninth Street for over seventy-two years. They're tearing down the building, so we came here on the advice of the O'Tooles who live on the seventh floor. Bless their souls, they have been a great help to us."

"Gee . . . it's . . . too bad . . . you . . . had to . . . leave . . . your . . . home."

"Do you always talk so slowly?" asked Zort, impatiently.

"Do . . . you . . . always . . . talk . . . so . . . fast?"

Zort reflected a moment "I see your point. Tell me a little about the Di Napoli family."

"There's not much to tell. Mr. Di Napoli . . . owns an . . . advertising firm . . . and makes a lot . . . of . . . money. Mrs. D . . . likes . . . to . . . buy . . . pocketbooks . . . and . . . matching . . . shoes. The children . . . are always into . . . mischief . . . and Nonno . . . that's Italian for . . . grandfather . . . he's a . . . jolly old . . . guy who . . . gets up during . . . the night . . . for a snack."

The last statement caused Zort some concern. "I'd better get moving. Don't want to be around when Nonno comes in. Good night . . . and thank you."

"Good . . . night." Hour Hand retreated into his shell as Zort hurried toward the kitchen, carrying his bag of tools.

Luckily, the door was slightly open. Zort slipped in cautiously, not knowing what to expect. All was quiet except for the hum of the refrigerator. The kitchen was spacious and perfectly in order. Zort's task was to determine what kind of food there was; how much of it there was; and how easy or difficult it would be to get food on a regular basis.

Like an acrobat, he leaped up to the counter that ran along the left wall just below a row of cabinets. The ability to make such leaps reflected the Wall People's exceptional strength and agility, qualities that were necessary for their survival. Zort opened his bag and pulled out a thick tube, which had a hook at one end. With rapid and well-practiced movements, he extended it like a telescope until it was more than five times his height. He lifted the pole, inserted the hook into a thin opening in a cabinet door, moved it as thought casting a fishing rod . . . and snap! The door swung open. In a few seconds Zort was investigating the contents of the cabinet.

What he found were dishes piled high and, hanging from hooks, dozens of flower-decorated cups.

"You guessed wrong," Zort told himself, as he walked briskly to another section, passing a large coffeepot, a section of glasses, huge mixing bowls and, finally, food . . . long, thin boxes whose labels read, fettuccini, linguini, lasagna . . . "I suppose we'll have to get used to eating Italian food," Zort mumbled matter-of-factly. Next to the boxes were cans of tomato paste and soup, boxes of cornmeal, a couple of loaves of sliced bread and a variety of other foods.

When he had completed his survey, Zort stood and scratched his head. "I don't see a blessed thing for my sweet tooth." He walked back to where his tools were, jumped down to the counter and looked around. He was just about convinced that there were no sweets around when he spotted it. Shaped like an old wine barrel: a large cookie jar.

"Sure enough, that'll satisfy my craving for sweets," he mused as he picked up his tools and headed for the other end of the counter. He couldn't reach the lid, so he hoppd up, balanced himself on the outer edge of the jar and, with some strain, lifted the ceramic cover. Holding it at arm's length, Zort looked in. There were only four heart-shaped cookies in the cavernous container. "I sure hope the usual supply is better than this," complained Zort. A split second later there was chaos.

He lost his footing.

He lost his hold on the cover.

Down he went.

Down went the cover with a bang, and Zort was trapped in the closed jar. Except for a scraped knee, Zort was not hurt. He sat up, felt around in the pitch dark, found his hat and placed it squarely on his head. Then suddenly, he heard someone speaking, and he froze with fear.

"Hello there. Hello there. *Buona sera. Buona sera.*"

The words were coming from inside the kitchen. "Hello there. *Buona sera.*"

There was something strange about the voice. It was not really like a human voice, more like a screech.

"A screech! Yes, a screech," Zort murmured. "It must be a parrot." That was a relief, but the noise would surely wake the family. Zort had to get out of his porcelain prison fast. He stood up and raised his arms; but even standing on his toes, he couldn't reach the top of the jar. His mind raced for a solution. There had to be a way out of the cookie jar. Then he remembered the cookies. He stacked them one on top of the other, climbed on the pile and was able to reach the top. Pushing with all his might, Zort slowly raised the cover and slid it to one side. With one great spring he was out and on the counter. But before he could catch his breath, the kitchen door swung open. Zort stiffened with fear. Certainly no parrot could have opened the door. Fortunately, it was only Mountain. The dog raised himself to the counter, his huge shaggy head and friendly brown eyes barely visible in the dim light.

"What's all the racket about? For a little man, you sure make a lot of noise."

"I assure you, Mountain, my normal *modus operandi* is shadowlike silence. But in this house my sainted grandmother's corpse would be forced to make noise."

"Hello there. *Buona sera,*" came the screeching voice.

"Speaking of noise, would you be so kind as to quiet that horrid bird?"

Mountain looked toward the far corner of the kitchen where a large cage, covered by a velvet cloth, stood.

"Oh, you mean Beeflat."

"Beeflat?" inquired Zort.

"Yeah. That's Mrs. D's name for her. Every time the bird screeches, Mrs. D says, 'She just hit B flat.' "

"Sounds normal for this house," observed Zort. "Now please shut her up."

"Sure, Zort. Anything to help."

Mountain lumbered across the room, placed his huge paws on the wall so that his head was level with the cage and growled. Beeflat instantly became silent.

"How did I do?" asked Mountain.

"You were superb. Now be a good dog and go back to sleep." Mountain obediently left the room.

"Let's see," said Zort, "where was I?" The night's unexpected encounters and confusion had made him lose his train of thought. He looked around. "Oh, yes . . . the refrigerator." He lowered his bag of tools with a rope and sprang from the counter. A moment later he was standing before the Di Napoli's refrigerator. Without hesitation he reached in his bag and pulled out an odd-looking tool. It was shaped like a duck's bill with a crank handle. He forced the tool behind the rubber seal of the refrigerator door and began turning the crank. In a few seconds the door opened and the refrigerator light went on, revealing a treasure of food. With a small rod propping the door open, Zort hopped in excitedly.

"Well, well, well . . . let's see now, what have we here?" He rubbed his hands briskly as he feasted his eyes on three quarts of milk. Wall People loved milk.

Look at that huge jar of peanut butter and those jams . . . excellent, excellent, thought Zort. The lower bins were filled with oranges, apples, lettuce, cucumbers and half dozen kinds of cheeses. At one point he came upon a long skinny sausage labeled "pepperoni." He studied it for some moments.

"Looks interesting," said Zort. Reaching into his jacket and pulling out a knife, he cut off a chunk and took a big bite. A few seconds later a roaring fire exploded in his mouth. His eyes teared. His mouth, tongue and throat burned intensely. It felt as though he had swallowed a white hot coal. Zort leaped out of the refrigerator, grabbed a plastic tube out of his bag and practically flew back to the upper shelf. Frantically he inserted the tube into a container of milk, operated a small hand pump and swallowed gulp after the gulp of milk. He was so involved that at first he did not sense the impending danger.

Someone was in the kitchen.

Not Rhinoceros.

Not Mountain.

Not Hour Hand.

It was one of the big people.

Almost too late, but with remarkable speed, Zort removed the rod from the door, the tube from the milk and hid behind the milk container. The refrigerator door swung open, and a huge face peered in. Large gray, compassionate eyes, white mustach and eyebrows. It was an old face, a wrinkled face, yet it seemed to be a friendly face.

This undoubtedly is Nonno, thought Zort. The old man's eyes darted around the shelves, trying to locate a good snack. Nothing appeared to appeal to him. He reached up and opened the door to the freezer, which containd several quarts of ice cream. He shook his head in disapproval. Then he began to survey the refrigerator again. A chubby hand reached in and grabbed a piece of chocolate cake.

Zort's heart was pounding wildly. "Surely he'll drink milk with the cake, and there goes my cover," he thought. He remained tense, waiting for the big hand to grab the milk. It was a moment of pure terror. Suddenly a familiar screeching voice broke the silence.

"Hello there. Hello there. *Buona sera. Buona sera.*"

The old man straightened up, turned, looked

toward the bird cage and began to mumble crossly. *"Ogni sera. Ogni sera. La stessa cosa."* (Every night. Every night. The same thing.) He waved his hand crossly at the bird, and his face flushed with anger at the thought of Beeflat announcing his presence in the kitchen to the whole family. *"Silenzio. Silenzio, uccello stupido."* (Quiet, quiet, stupid bird.)

Zort took the opportunity, while Nonno was distracted, to race up the door shelves and hide behind a large container of ice cream in the freezer, which had no light. A moment later all was quiet. A chubby hand reached into the refrigerator and grabbed the container of milk, followed by the sound of liquid pouring into a glass. Then the hand replaced the milk on the shelf. A second later everything went black as the freezer and the refrigerator doors slammed shut.

Zort's keen hearing told him Nonno was leaving the kitchen. Just to be safe, he remained still for a few more minutes, though he began to feel bitterly cold. "I should have put on an overcoat," he whispered.

The darkness made the cold seem worse. Finally, Zort left his hiding place. One careful step after another brought him to the freezer door. He leaned against it and pushed with all the strength he could muster. The door remained closed.

Three . . . four . . . five times he tried. It would not budge, and he did not have any of his tools. Zort had a sudden surge of fear, a crushing feeling of helplessness. How long could he endure the numbing cold? Eventually one of the big people would find him . . . then what? He sat down to think things out. There had to be an answer to this predicament. The words of a song that his mother often sang came to him: "If a mountain is blocking your path to a star, there's always another way."

A flood of memories raced through his mind: Memories of his mother, his nephew, great-nephews and nieces . . . a century and a quarter of living in New York. It seemed absurd that Zort W. Calabash, the patriarch of the Wall People, should end his life in the Di Napoi's refrigerator. For nearly an hour he tried without success to open the door.

Then he decided to try his mental power. He squeezed his face as tightly as he could and concentrated on the door. Nothing happened. He tried again. Still nothing. His power for moving objects by mental concentration was not always consistent. So he decided to try using his mental powers in another way.

Zort concentrated on a distress message. Perhaps Krim, his nephew, would receive it through mental telepathy. He kept the message flowing for several minutes. But it was difficult to concentrate because of the unbearable cold.

Gradually Zort began feeling drowsy, a bad sign. People become sleepy just before freezing to death. He tried staying awake, yet sleep seemed so pleasant. His last thoughts were of the clan waiting in the ceiling space. Who would take care of them? Who would . . . even his thoughts faded. Finally, his body went limp, lying motionless in the dark freezer.

A strange feeling greeted Zort when he opened his eyes. He was wearing his overcoat and being fed Irish whiskey.

"Uncle Zort, Uncle Zort, say something," a young voice pleaded.

As consciousness slowly returned, Zort realized that Krim was holding him and that Frollin, Krim's oldest son, was briskly rubbing his hands to increase his circulation.

Krim, his nephew, was a sandy-haired young man of slender frame, standing just under five inches in height. Unlike Zort, he was effervescent and almost always cheerful. He loved to read poetry to his children and, on occasion, when the big people were away, dance a lively jig.

His son Frollin, in many ways, seemed to be the complete opposite. He seldom ever spoke and had come to be known as "the quiet one." He was rather short for his age, but had a broad, powerful frame. Although he spoke very seldom, when he did speak, one immediately realized that Frollin was intelligent and sensitive.

"Praise be to the Lord," sighed Zort. "You received my message."

"It came through loud and clear," said Krim with a broad smile. "We'll have you back with the clan in a few minutes. For a while we thought we had lost you."

Supported by Krim and Frollin, Zort made his way across the kitchen, through the dining room and across the living room, to a beautiful china closet in the corner of the room. They walked beneath the closet to the wall. Krim tapped twice . . . twice again, then three rapid taps. From what seemed to be solid woodwork, there appeared a miniature doorway. It was a specially crafted doorway, carefully cut out by the wall people to provide access to the apartment. A single doorway took as long as two months to produce. It was done with such skill that it was nearly invisible to the naked eye.

They entered a dark, cavelike area, and a small figure in a ruffled skirt quickly closed the door. In sharp contrast to the Di Napolis' luxurious living room, the world of the walls was drab, barren and dark. No light ever entered these spaces. No sunlight ever warmed the dusty beams that ran vertically and horizontally to form the skeleton of the walls. The musty smell of dry plaster made the narrow area feel even more confining. In the summer it was unbearably hot and in the winter, numblingly cold.

"Uncle Zort!" a delicate, bell-like voice cried softly. "Are you all right?"

"He'll be fine, Alba," answered Krim.

"Don't worry about me, child. It'll take far more than a stuck refrigerator to do in your Uncle Zort."

There was a momentary flash of a match, and a lantern came to life, revealing a petite woman with golden hair set in long braids, fair skin and green eyes. Like all women in the clan, Alba wore bright clothes: a yellow skirt and a red blouse with a yellow collar.

Supported by Krim and Frollin, Zort began to ascend a wooden ladder. They were met at the top by the other anxious members of the clan: Zort's white-haired mother, Krim's younger son, Vand, and his two daughters, Starlight and Buttercup. Zort had now regained most of his strength. For an hour he sat on a mattress with the clan gathered around him, telling them about the events of the evening: his encounters with Rhinoceros, Mountain, Hour Hand and Beeflat. The children's eyes widened as he described his close call with Nonno and his entombment in the refrigerator. At the end of his tale, no one said a word. The group of little people just watched the patriarch, each cheerful face wearing a question mark. Had they found a new home?

Zort got up and stood tall. He adjusted his top hat. Then he spoke.

"To be sure, now I can see that you all want to know if we've found a new home. Well . . . I'll tell you. I'd be the devil's own liar if I said this was paradise. The Di Napolis' house is far from the ideal, quiet, undisturbed, orderly and predictable place we would prefer. Common sense would dictate our moving to another, more stable house, where our chances for a peaceful, tranquil life, or at least for survival, would be reasonable. But things are not always what they seem to be."

"Ah, come on, Uncle Zort," said Krim, his large brown eyes twinkling with a warm smile. "Are we staying or aren't we?"

Zort looked at seven pairs of pleading eyes. Then he looked around. The space between floors was ten inches high. Zort liked high ceilings. There was sixteen inches between beams, so the rooms would be spacious. They'd be able to connect into the chimney for the stove, he thought.

"Well . . . 'tis going to be very interesting, to say the least . . . and I'll probably live to regret it . . . however . . ." He extended his long arms as if to enfold the entire clan. ". . . it's a grand feeling I have to be telling you that it looks as though we've got a new home."

In a comfortable corner of the living room, looking like a huge bundle of furs, Mountain lay sleeping. Suddenly he raised his head, perked up his floppy ears and looked around. He couldn't be sure, but he thought he heard a group of little voices cheering.

2 ✽ Where's Buttercup

It was 3:00 p.m. After a good long sleep and an adequate breakfast, thanks to the generosity of the O'Tooles, the clan was ready and eager to get to work. The feeling of excitement was evident as everyone gathered around Zort waiting for instructions. Setting up a home was a new experience for them. Wall People never moved to a new location unless it was absolutely necessary. Except for Zort and his mother, the Calabash family had lived in the 89th Street home all their lives.

29

Now they had to make new living quarters. They felt like pioneers. Their faces reflected a determination to make their new ceiling space the most beautiful of all the Wall People.

Zort cleared his throat and began to address them in his usual formal manner. " 'Tis a happy clan indeed I see assembled before me, a clan with full intentions to work hard and get a great deal accomplished. But, what we need is organization." He raised a finger to his temple to stress his point. "Organization is vital to the success of any project."

"Well, what is it you'd have us do! Lord knows, 'tis no time for making a speech," complained Zort's mother, half teasing.

"Patience, Mother, patience. Remember there is great virtue in patience. Now let's see, where was I?" Zort paused a moment.

"As you all know, this is going to be a very busy day for us. There's a great deal to be done just so this place will be fit to lay our weary bones down. Lord knows 'twill be years before we can really call it a home."

" 'Twas many a year that passed before we finished with the building of our darlin' home on Eighty-ninth Street," added Zort's mother.

"Besides the bringing up of furniture from the basement and fixin' up here," continued Zort, "Krim and I still have to go back to the old place this evening to get the stove and the last of our belongings. So there is no time to waste. Before I give you your assignment, has anyone checked the vapor bowls?"

"Good heavens, yes!" answered Alba firmly. "Do you think we'd ever let the vapor bowls go out? Lord knows what's crawling around in these walls."

The vapor bowls were crucial to the Wall People's survival. Each bowl was filled with a powder that burned like incense, covering an area of about ten feet around with a scent that was thoroughly repugnant to all sorts of crawling insects and rodents. The powder, which had been developed centuries earlier in Ireland, was a strange mixture of ground-up pits from fruits, paint chips, various spices and a number of ingredients known only to those members of the Wall People called "the chemists," who specialized in the art of mixing herbs and chemicals. There was usually at least one chemist in each building occupied by clans.

"Fine, Alba. I was just checking," said Zort. "What was I about to say?" he murmured. "Oh yes. Here's the way we'll break up the work. Krim, you drill the hole in the chimney wall for the stove. Frollin, you and Vand go down to the O'Tooles' and fetch the floor boards. Ask Mr. O'Toole and his son Patrick to help you. We'll need to lay them down before we can bring up the furniture."

At the mention of Patrick O'Toole, Starlight's eyes lit up and the slightest trace of color flushed her normally pale face.

"Mother," said Zort, "you can begin dusting and cleaning around this area."

"I didn't need the likes of you to tell me that this place needed a good sweepin'," snapped his mother, goodnaturedly.

"Alba," continued Zort with the slightest trace of a smile, "you and Starlight string up the wires for the room divider drapes. It'll be a year before we have the walls up."

"Naturally, I will be available to assist all of you with your chores.

"Are there any questions?"

"What about me," asked Buttercup.

Zort stared down at his little niece. She looked like a doll, dressed in a bright yellow dress with green polka dots and matching yellow bows at the ends of her braids. "Hmmmm. What will your job be?" he mused.

"Well, what can I do?" she repeated with childish impatience.

"I know. You will be my official assistant."

"You mean it?" asked Buttercup excitedly.

"That I do," answered Zort as he looked around. "All right. Let's get started," he instructed with a clap of his hands.

Everyone swung into action, applying themselves energetically to their tasks.

Buttercup drifted away from Zort after a few minutes, fascinated by the variety of activity, especially the work her father was doing. Krim was using a hand operated drill to make a hole in the brick wall. His task would require many hours of tedious labor. Boring through twelve inches of mortar was a huge task.

Buttercup watched quietly for a few seconds. Then she gave in to her irresistible curiosity. "What are you doing, Father?"

"Making a hole in the chimney, sweetheart."

"How come it's such a small hole?" she asked, placing her smooth cheek next to her father's and staring into the hole.

"First I make a small hole. Then I make it larger. It's easier that way," Krim answered patiently.

"How does the drill work?"

Krim put the tool down, placed both hands on Buttercup's shoulders and kissed her on the tip of her nose. "Sweetheart, that precious little head of yours will never run out of questions. And your father will never get the hole drilled. And the stove will never be put in. And we'll never get a cooked meal."

Buttercup's face broke into a devilish smile, and her large brown eyes twinkled. She put her small hand on his face. "You want me to go away, Father?"

Krim smiled and gave her a hug. "Just find yourself a little corner and play with your doll."

Buttercup gave her father a kiss, walked away, stopping to watch each member of the family at work. Finally she caught up with Zort and tugged on his pants leg. "Great-Uncle Zort, tell me more about Mountain. He sounds nice. I love him already. Can I meet him, please, can I meet him?"

"Certainly not. Now be still and just watch."

"Move it over a little to the right, Alba," he called out. Alba and Starlight were stringing wires across from one beam to another. From these they would hang drapes that would act as room dividers to form a series of sleeping rooms. A large area next to the chimney wall was set aside for the family room. This comprised the kitchen, living room and dining room.

A series of large boards would also be placed across the rough floor to provide a smooth surface. The present surface was a series of dry plaster lumps, which had been forced through the lath when the big people's apartment's ceiling had been made. The boards would also block all light from the Wall People's home, thereby preventing it from being seen by the big people. Rugs would be placed over the boards.

In time the drape room dividers would be replaced by regular walls, which would be painted bright colors.

Buttercup tried as hard as she could and didn't say a word for at least two minutes. That was her limit.

"What are the wires for?"

"Sure now, you'd wear out the patience of St. Francis himself. Did I not just ask you to be quiet?"

"I thought I was your official assistant."

"You are."

"Can I give orders to everyone like you do?"

"No!"

"Why not."

"Because you're not ready for that."

"I am too," insisted Buttercup.

Zort squatted down and stared at his little niece. "Young lady. You won't understand this, but I will say it anyway. One doesn't give orders just because one likes to give them. One must recognize the necessity of following orders before exercising the responsibility of giving them."

Buttercup wrinkled her nose, stared blankly at him and walked away giggling. She wandered around for a few minutes, watching Frollin and Vand struggle with some large boards. Then she spotted an opportunity to help. Alba and Starlight had finished stringing up the wires and were hanging a large drape on one of them.

They were up on ladders trying to hook it to the wire and pull it across. Buttercup grabbed the bottom of the drape and pulled as hard as she could. It was the wrong thing to do.

"No, no, no! Stop pulling," scolded Alba frantically from her ladder. But in her enthusiasm, Buttercup did not listen and pulled even harder.

Everything seemed to happen at once.

The few hooks holding the heavy drape disconnected. Alba and Starlight tried to grab it, but it slipped from their grips. Unfortunately, Frollin and Vand were below, holding a large floor board on end. More unfortunately, Zort was standing there in deep meditation.

The drape fell, covering Frollin and Vand. They, in turn, lost their balance and, still holding onto the heavy floorboard, fell onto Zort, while Buttercup managed to scamper out of the way, suddenly aware that she had just created a horrendous situation.

What followed was a tangle of confusion. Vand, with a sheepish grin, was the first to emerge from the folds of the drape, followed by a very annoyed Frollin. The drape and floorboard were quickly lifted from the clan patriarch, who sprang to his feet, livid with indignation. His top hat was crushed, his jacket wrinkled and his hair sticking straight out. He looked as if he had just come out of an eggbeater. Everyone waited for

Zort's verbal explosion, but could barely keep from laughing at the hilarious sight.

Zort just stood there quivering. Then he took three deep breaths, smoothed his hair down, brushed the wrinkles out of his jacket, and punched his top hat back into reasonable shape. "My dear niece . . . I value my clothes, especially my top hat. But I value my life even more. Is it unreasonable of me to expect you to see that your offspring do not become the cause of our total destruction? Please see that Buttercup does not threaten our safety again."

"Yes, Uncle Zort," answered Alba timidly.

"Would ya listen to him," said Grandma. "One would think all the bones in his body were broken. Don't be frettin', son. I'm sure they'll all be more careful not ta damage your delicate frame," she added with a smile.

"Fine. Now, let us all resume our chores. There's still a lot of work to be done."

Buttercup was snuggling close to her mother when Grandma walked over and put her arms around the child. "There, there, little angel, come on with Grandma. We'll stay out of the way of the cranky grown-ups. Alba, you go about your work. Buttercup and I will be fine."

The clan resumed their routine, putting down floor boards, laying out rugs, assembling bed frames, moving furniture into place and a dozen other chores.

Grandma sat in her favorite easy chair, a hand-carved rocker that her husband had made for her nearly a hundred and thirty years before. Buttercup crawled up on her lap. "Now there, child, what shall we talk about?"

Buttercup hesitated awhile, holding her doll, Wiggles, closely. Then her eyes lit up. "Tell Wiggles and me all about the old country and how the Wall People got started."

"But I've told you that story many times before."

"Oh, please tell it again. We just love to hear it."

"No one is exactly sure, but according to my father, rest his soul, and his father, our clan goes all the way back to the fifth century in Ireland, during the time of St. Patrick."

"That's the old country, isn't it?"

" 'Tis the old country for sure."

"The old country is beautiful isn't it?"

"Child, there is beauty there that a soul cannot find anywhere else in the world. Well, as I started to say, the way I heard it told, there was a small community of people who lived up in the corner of Ireland, a place where, it is said, a great many volcanoes erupted for thousands of years, long before anyone lived in the area. It's called Derry. That's where the O'Hagarty and the McClosky clans come from.

"This small community lived quietly. But something about them was strange. All the people were rather small. Not tiny like us. But smaller than usual."

"How small were they, Grandma?"

"Well, now, child, 'tis hard to say. But suppose most of the people in that time were about five and a half feet tall, these people were perhaps a bit over four feet. Not midgets, but very short, as people go. And each generation got even smaller. My father believed that there must have been special vapors coming out of the ground in the area that affected the people."

"You mean like our vapor bowls?"

"Sure now, let's hope that our vapor bowls are not making us any smaller than we are. But whatever these vapors were, about two hundred years later, the people had gotten so small that they dared not be seen by outsiders. Luckily, some of them were not as much affected, and they were the ones who would travel to far-off towns to buy supplies. But eventually they died, and the little people were left alone. To lessen their chances of being seen by other humans, or "the big people," as regular people came to be known, the community migrated westward and settled in the Twelve Bens."

"The Twelve Bens?" asked Buttrcup.

"Yes, darlin'. They're twelve tall mountains

around the area of Galway Bay. Anyway, the community of little people lived as best they could for a few hundred years, learning all the things they needed to know in order to survive."

"Oh, how exciting. What did they do next? How did they start living in cities? How did they get to New York?"

"Wait up. Wait up, child." Grandma, laughed, hugging Buttercup and kissing her on the top of her head. "So many questions for such a little head."

"But I want to know," insisted Buttercup.

"It'll have to wait. I've got chores to do. Now you be a good girl and sit in this comfortable chair with Wiggles." A moment later, the old lady was busy at work. For the next few hours all went smoothly.

Krim was well along with drilling the first hole. Frollin and Vand had laid down all the floor boards. Alba and Starlight had hung most of the drapes. Zort had supervised the work with the precision and authority of an experienced general. And finally Alba could pause at the top of a ladder to relax for a moment. Nearby on the other ladder Starlight took the cue from her mother and also paused in her work.

"Well now, that takes care of that drape. Only two more to go," said Alba, with a sense of pride.

"Mother, I think this is going to be really a nice place to live. There's something very likeable about it."

"You mean likeable about him," teased Alba. "I saw your eyes light up when we met the O'Toole boy."

Starlight's face became crimson, and she lowered her eyes.

"Oh darlin', I didn't mean to embarrass you. He seems like a fine lad." Alba paused a moment. "I know how lonesome you were on Eighty-ninth Street. There was no one to your likin' in the building. But don't be worrying yourself to a frazzle. You're a beautiful and intelligent young lady, and before you know it a half-dozen young men in this buildin' will come courtin'."

Starlight didn't answer, but simply smiled at her mother.

"We'd better get going on the other drapes if we're to have a little privacy tonight!" exclaimed Alba. "We ought to be finished with the drapes in a half-hour, that is, if we don't get any help from Buttercup. Speaking of that little imp, she's been awfully quiet; too quiet, in fact. I wonder what she's up to."

"Buttercup," she called out. There was no answer.

"Buttercup," she called louder. Alba hur-

ried down the ladder calling, "Buttercup, Buttercup."

"Buttercup," she cried out.

Krim, Frollin and Vand ran over.

"What's wrong?"

"Buttercup. I can't find her."

"Calm down," said Krim. "There are dozens
of corners and spaces around here where she
could be playing or hiding." They all began to
fan out calling Buttercup. But there was no re-
sponse. Eventually, they were joined by Grandma
and Zort. But Buttercup was nowhere around.

Alba was on the verge of tears. "Has anyone seen Buttercup?" she pleaded.

"She was with me. But that was a few hours
ago," answered Grandma.

"Now don't panic," counseled Zort. "We'll
find her."

Everyone began to search the area again,
without success. A mood of desperation gripped
the clan.

"Could she have strayed beyond the vapor
bowls?" asked Vand.

"No," answered Krim. "Even Buttercup
knows better than to do that."

Nevertheless, Krim, Zort and Frollin ven-
tured beyond the protection of the vapor bowls
to search. They climbed over beams, around large
water pipes, drain pipes and around electrical

junction boxes and indentations of brick work, but to no avail.

"Oh, God, where's my little girl?" cried Alba, trying desperately to control her emotions.

"It's my fault," sobbed Grandma. "Everyone had chased her away. She begged me to tell her more stories. And I was too busy."

"Now let's not go blaming ourselves about something we're not even sure has happened," said Zort sternly, but with a worried look.

❋   ❋   ❋

He blended with the shadows like a dark evil spirit. His name was Black Jack, and he was as evil as any human being had ever been. Quietly, without even seeming to breathe, the lonely figure stood in an unlit doorway across the street from an elegant apartment building on the corner of 85th Street and Park Avenue.

Tonight was the night. He had reviewed his plan a hundred times, and soon it would be time to strike. As usual, he was dressed in solid black: black turtleneck sweater, hat, jacket, trousers, sharp pointed shoes, even black gloves. His face was thin and bony. His hair was combed straight back, and his sinister eyes, long nose and jaw and thin-lined mouth seemed all too appropriate to his slender, spiderlike body.

Black Jack looked at his watch. The luminous dial read 7:15. He shot a quick glance across the street. Hurrying down 85th Street like a lumbering hippopotamus was a short, broad-shouldered man in his mid-thirties, built like a human bulldozer. Black Jack called him Zero, because in Black Jack's opinion, he had no intelligence at all.

"Okay, boss," Zero reported with a great sense of pride, "I got a poifect parkin' spot . . . right across da street from da side of da buildin'. Another guy was gonna take the spot, but I told him, I was gonna break him in two if he didn't beat it. How was that boss . . . okay?"

"You fool," Black Jack hissed. "I told you not to do anything that would cause the slightest trouble." He paused for a few seconds and looked in the direction of the car. The block was deserted, even though it was still early and an exceptionally warm evening for mid-December. Jack lookd up. "We're going to have a storm tonight. That's good, very good. Less of a chance for people to be in the streets."

He looked at Zero. "Now don't forget all the things I told you. I want everything to go smooth tonight, no slip ups."

"Don't worry boss, I didn't forget anything."

"Good! Now be back at two o'clock and stay in the car, out of sight."

"Right boss."

Black Jack watched him walk down the street, then he glanced at the luxury building in which the Di Napolis lived. An evil smile broke the straight thin line of his mouth. "I'll be back," he whispered as he slipped into the shadows. "The Di Napolis have a lot of goodies, just waiting for me to pick." A moment later he vanished into the night.

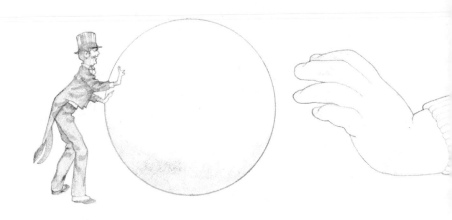

3 ✳ Mountain's New Friend

At 7:30 p.m. the Di Napoli family was relaxing in the grand living room. Delicate threads of light reflected off the gold and silver Christmas garland hanging on the marble stairway winding up to a balcony that extended around two walls.

John Di Napoli sat comfortably on a large couch in front of a marble fireplace with his feet propped up on the coffee table, sipping brandy and reading the newspaper. Mrs. Di Napoli sat next to him leafing through a magazine, casually flipping pages. Nonno sat in his favorite chair, his shirtsleeves rolled up, devouring every word of his Italian newspaper, *Il Progresso.*

The children were having fun rolling a ball back and forth across the floor, trying to knock down a number of blocks set up in the middle of the room. For a while Julie had unsuccessfully tried to get Mountain interested in the rolling ball, hoping he would scramble for it and join their fun. But the young St. Bernard lay in the corner, under the baby grand piano, with his head resting on his paws.

Julie was a picture of her mother; long dark brown hair and sparkling, cheerful eyes. Joey had his father's stamp; husky, light-eyed and good-natured.

"Look at dumb ole Mountain; he won't play with us at all," said Julie.

"Maybe he's tired," suggested Joey.

"From what? He hasn't done a dumb ole thing all day except go for a dumb ole walk. And he's been lying in that dumb ole corner all evening." Julie suddenly rolled the ball toward the corner of the room. It stopped between Mountain's outstretched paws. The dog didn't move.

"There you see? Nothing. I don't know what's wrong with him," she said, walking over and picking up the ball. "Do you think he's sick?"

"Yeah," answered Joey, laughing. "Sick of you."

"Smarty."

The children resumed their game, deciding to ignore Mountain. After a few minutes, Julie looked up at her father.

"Daddy."

"Don't ask," he said without even putting down his paper.

"But you don't even know what I was going to say," she complained.

"You were going to ask about Christmas, about the Christmas tree. Right?"

"It's so close to Christmas, and we don't have our tree yet."

"Young lady, it is exactly two weeks before Christmas. If we put up a tree now, it will dry out by Christmas and look all droopy. I tell you what. We'll get the tree this Saturday. That's only two days more. And we'll decorate it on Sunday. Is that fair enough?"

"Oh! I'm so excited, I can't wait," squealed Julie. "Too bad it's so warm. It doesn't even seem like Christmas."

"Don't worry, precious," said Mrs. Di Napoli. "I just heard the weather report. We're supposed to have a freak rainstorm tonight, with thunder and lightning, and sometime during the night the temperature is supposed to drop all the way into the twenties. You never can tell, the rain might change into snow before morning."

"You think so, you really think so?" asked both children almost in unison.

"You watcha, it's a-snow tonight," interrupted Nonno. He was rubbing his left elbow. "Whena my arma hurt, shesa gonna snow."

❄   ❄   ❄

Holding a small lamp, Krim and Zort made their way down a long wooden ladder as the rest of the clan looked on. The lantern light cast hideous shadows along the walls of the narrow space. As soon as the light was out of sight, Alba turned to the others. "I pray the good Lord is watching over Buttercup, where ever my baby is," she cried.

"Don't worry, Mother," consoled Starlight. "I'm sure she's down at the O'Tooles'. You know how she loves to visit people."

Grandma sat silently, one hand to her face, the other holding Buttercup's doll, tears streaming down her cheeks. After what seemed to be an eternity, they heard the men returning, the light bobbing sideways as the two figures climbed at a slow pace. Soon they were standing before the clan. Their grim faces told the story.

"She's not at the O'Tooles'," said Krim in a discouraged voice.

Alba embraced her husband, sobbing pitifully. "My Buttercup. My precious little baby. Where is she? Dear Lord, where is she?"

Suddenly Zort had an idea. "Wait a minute!" he said, snapping his finger. "I think I know where she might be."

Zort turned to Alba. "Did you lock the entrance door to the Di Napolis' last night?"

Albo hesitated. "I don't know. I can't remember. There was so much excitement. What with you being nearly killed. I don't rightly know."

She thought a moment more. Then her eyes widened with a look of shock and terror. "You don't think she wandered into the Di Napoli apartment?"

Zort nodded his head.

"But they're still up and about. She'll be seen, or stepped on, or killed by one of the animals." She placed her hand to her mouth and looked at Krim.

"There's no time to waste," said Zort in a commanding voice. "Come on, Krim. We're going down there."

A few minutes later they were descending the ladder again.

The patriarch and his nephew stopped and listened at the entrance. They could hear talking. Julie was once again taunting Mountain for being so lazy and refusing to move from his spot.

The door was unlocked.

"Are you ready," whispered Zort.

"I guess so," answered Krim. "What are we going to do when we go in?"

"We'll figure out what to do when we get in there."

Zort gripped the knob of the door, opened it a crack and looked into the living room. He could see Mr. and Mrs. Di Napoli sitting on a couch and could only hear Julie. The couch was blocking her from his view.

Zort opened the door a bit more, enough to poke his head out. To his right he could see Joey sitting opposite his sister. Mountain was curled up, like a giant furry ball, in the corner under the baby grand piano.

"I don't see her," he whispered to Krim.

"Maybe she's in another room."

"Could be. We'll have to make it past the Di Napoli's to get to the dining room." They silently slipped into the room, hidden in the deep shadowed area beneath the china closet, and studied the situation.

"The boy is right in our way. We'll never get past him," whispered Krim.

"We'll have to wait. Maybe he'll move to get the ball," suggested Zort.

The children rolled the ball back and forth, laughing as the blocks in the center of the room tumbled down. At one point Julie threw the ball very hard, and it bounced off Joey's foot rolling dangerously close to the china closet. Zort and Krim flattened themselves against the wall behind one of the legs. But Joey got the ball before it rolled under the closet, while Julie was once again calling Mountain a "dumb ole dog."

"This will never do," said Zort. "We've got to think of something."

"There doesn't seem to be any other way of getting around them," whispered Krim. "We'd have to walk past the entire family to get to the dining room door."

"There is another way . . . Mountain."

"I don't get it."

"If we can get Mountain to come here, we can hide in his fur and have him carry us into the dining room."

"How are you going to get him to come here?" asked Krim.

"That's the problem. We'll have to get his attention."

Zort stepped out from behind the china closet leg and looked at Mountain. The dog's large, shaggy head was resting between his paws, his brown eyes following the ball from one side of the room to another.

Zort waited until the ball was halfway across the room, then started waving his long arms. Mountain caught sight of the little man. His ears perked up, and he raised his head. Zort

made a great effort to get the huge dog to come
to them. He even used his mental powers to make
Mountain understand how desperately they
needed him. But the St. Bernard wouldn't budge
from his spot. Either he had not gotten the message, or he had lost all interest in Zort. Several
times, as the ball rolled by, the little man waved
his arms and made every possible motion to get
Mountain to come to the china closet. But all his
efforts were in vain.

"It's no use," whispered Zort. "The little
girl is perfectly right. He is a dumb ole dog."

"Watch out," warned Krim, pulling his
uncle's arm violently. A moment later a large
ball came rolling by and settled against the wall,
blocking the door to the wall space.

"What'll we do Uncle Zort? The boy is coming to get the ball. He'll see us for sure."

Once again they flattened themselves as
tightly as they could against the wall behind the
wooden leg of the closet and held their breaths.
Suddenly a chubby hand reached under the
closet and began feeling around. It was inches
away from the two small people. Krim's heart
was pounding; beads of sweat rolled down his
brow. At any moment that big hand could come
crashing against them.

As usual Zort acted with speed. He moved
sideways, put both arms around the ball and

managed to roll it against Joey's searching hand. Five pudgy fingers grasped the ball, and a moment later it was gone.

"Whew! That was close," said Krim. You certainly have a quick mind."

"I've been in a lot worse spots than that," answered his uncle matter-of-factly.

"Okay. Time for bed," came a voice from the balcony, one unknown to Zort. It was a voice with a strong brogue, the sound of someone newly come from Ireland.

"Let's go, darlin's. Sure now, your little bodies are needin' some rest, so's you'll be bright and chipper tomorrow at school."

There was the sound of heavy footsteps as someone descended the steps to the dining room.

"Ah, ten minutes more, Ma," complained Joey. "We're having so much fun."

"I'm afraid not, sweetheart," answered Mary Di Napoli. "It's eight fifteen. You're supposed to be in the tub by eight."

"Ah, come on, Mommy," begged Julie. "We never get to stay up late."

"I tell you what, in two weeks your Christmas vacation begins, I'll let you stay up until ten o'clock every night. How's that?"

"Super," said Joey. "But can we play for five minutes more?"

"No," said Mrs. Di Napoli firmly, and the two children sighed and started up the stairs to their bedrooms. Julie looked over the banister at Mountain. He was still in the same spot, with his head between his paws and his eyes fixed on the children.

"I hope you get all wrinkly, dumb ole dog. You sure were no fun tonight."

"Come on, now. Off to your baths with you," ordered Mrs. O'Callighan. A few seconds later they disappeared into their rooms.

"How would everyone like a nice fresh cup of coffee?" asked Mrs. Di Napoli. "And there's still some of that great chocolate cake left."

"Fine," agreed Mr. D. and Nonno.

"Let's have it in the kitchen. Dora just vacuumed the living room, and she'll have a fit if we get crumbs all over the rug." She got up and walked out of the room, followed a few minutes later by her husband and father.

Finally, the living room was perfectly empty except for Mountain. Zort waved his arms and called out softly to the dog. Perhaps he might know something about Buttercup's whereabouts. It was important to get all the information possible before venturing into the room while the big people were still up and about.

Once again Mountain perked up his ears, raised his head and looked toward the china closet. But then he muzzled his nose into the soft long fur near his back leg.

"What a time to be biting fleas," groaned

Zort. "Sure now, 'tis the dumbest animal the good Lord has ever created. Let's go over to him."

"No," answered Krim. "Look! Look! I can't believe my eyes." From out of his long fur, the big St. Bernard had picked up a tiny little figure by the back of her dress, as delicately as a mother picking up a newborn puppy. Dangling happily from Mountain's mouth was none other than Buttercup.

Krim could barely control himself, he was so happy. He wanted to shout for joy and dash from the hiding place. But he waited as the loveable animal plodded across the living room, lay down before the china closet and snuggled his nose beneath the furniture, allowing Buttercup to drop gently into her father's outstretched arms.

"Daddy, Daddy, I met Mountain. He's my friend. He saved me from the big people and from Rhinoceros."

Zort stepped forward and patted Mountain on his soft nose. "My friend, you have, indeed, been of great service to us. In the name of all the Wall People, I thank you."

"Did I really help?"

"You averted a great tragedy for us all."

Zort patted Mountain on the nose once more and said good night. Alba, Grandma and the others stood nervously as they heard Zort and

Krim ascending the ladder. Soon Buttercup popped her head up and was immediately lifted into her mother's arms. The sense of joy and excitement at the return of Buttercup bordered on pandemonium. Buttercup was passed from one set of arms to another.

Finally Buttercup caught her breath and described her experience. "Oh, Mommy, I met Mountain. He's my friend. I love him, and he saved me from the big people," she rattled off without taking a breath. "I was in the big people's living room looking for Mountain. It was fun walking through the carpet. I saw all the beautiful furniture. It's so big," she marveled.

"How did you end up in Mountain's fur?" asked her father.

Fully enjoying being the center of attention, Buttercup became very dramatic in describing her adventure. "There I was," she began, "walking around the living room, all alone. Then I saw this big, ferocious animal crouched on the other side of the room. It was making a scary sound and looking at me in a strange way. I knew that it must be Rhinoceros."

Buttercup looked around to be sure that everyone was watching her. "I was terribly scared.

"Then Rhinoceros started at me. I didn't know which way to run. All I could think of was being eaten up by the beast." With those words, Alba embraced her little girl, held her tight and kissed her head.

Buttercup wiggled free. "Mommy, Mommy, let me tell you what happened next," she said as everyone laughed. Buttercup continued. "All of a sudden, a giant animal, a whole lot bigger than the one coming at me, ran into the room, saw me, and began to growl at the cat. I knew at once that the big animal was Mountain. He growled so ferociously that Rhinoceros ran to another room. As soon as Mountain looked down at me, I knew that he was my friend. He lowered his head and let me pat his big wet nose.

"Just then I heard the big people coming toward the living room. Mountain knew that they shouldn't see me. So he picked me up, ran over to the corner of the room and tucked me safely in his fur. I was so scared, but I knew that Mountain wouldn't let anything bad happen to me. While I was waiting, I could hear the big people talking and the girl calling Mountain a dumb ole dog. I felt so bad for poor Mountain."

"Well now, young lady," said Zort, "I certainly hope that you have learned a lesson from this. You could have easily been killed or captured by the big people."

Suddenly Buttercup remembered something. "Oh, I forgot! The big people are going to get their Christmas tree this Saturday. Can we put up a little tree too . . . please, Daddy, can we . . . and we can decorate it with all our beautiful Christmas balls."

"As soon as we can, we'll get a small branch from their tree and decorate it together," Krim answered her. Everyone laughed and talked. Starlight began to sing a Christmas carol, and a wonderful feeling of happiness settled on the Calabash clan.

Down in the quiet living room Mountain lay with his nose under the china closet for a long while. From the tiny sounds he knew that his little friends were very happy. It made him feel warm and wonderful inside.

4 ✳ Dangerous Journey
to 89th Street

The Calabash Clan was still brimming over with merriment when Zort made an announcement. He cleared his throat to get their attention. "Far be it from me to put a damper on such a joyous occasion, but may I remind my nephew that there's still an important task to accomplish."

"You're ready to leave for the old place?" asked Krim.

"Precisely," Zort answered. "We must pick up the last of our belongings."

"Must you go tonight?" asked Zort's mother. "You've had such a hard day. Sure now, tomorrow you'll be well rested."

"They'll be starting demolition tomorrow. We won't get another chance."

A serious mood settled over the group. A trip to the old house would be dangerous, even at this late hour. Grandma placed her hand on her son's arm. "Darlin', I get heartsick thinkin' of you and Krim out there in the street, easy prey to man and beast. Couldn't we forget about what's in the old house?"

"Forget? Mother, do you know now what it is you're saying? It took years for us to accumulate the things for the house. We need them all, especially the stove."

"Well." She sighed. "What's to be done will be done. Be careful. We almost had one tragedy; Lord knows, we don't want another."

"Don't worry, Grandma," said Krim, placing his arm around her. "With Uncle Zort we're always in safe hands."

For the next half-hour they planned the trip. Krim put on black clothes and a black hood. Even Zort made a rare exception and replaced his white dress shirt with a black one. They checked their ropes, pulleys and tools and were finally ready to leave.

Down the long ladder went Zort and his

nephew, while a group of anxious faces watched. Krim paused for a moment and looked up; he could still see Alba's outline.

"Come on, Krim. No time to stop now."

"Coming, Uncle." He hurried down the ladder.

It was a long climb, but they were capable of moving with great speed—past the Di Napoli apartment on the fourteenth floor and the Bushmanns' on the tenth. They stopped at the O'Tooles' on the seventh floor to get some extra rope.

The O'Tooles had lived in this building for the past sixty years and knew every inch of the structure. Over the six decades they had fabricated a comfortable home with a large combination kitchen, dining room, living room, with a fireplace built into the building's chimney, a stove and even a small wood-burning heating stove for cold winter nights. Their home had a large bedroom for Mr. and Mrs. O'Toole, one for Patrick and his younger brother Lydin and another bedroom for Breeza, the O'Tooles' beautiful daughter. They even had a guest room, so they could offer hospitality to a visitor from another building.

Zort had stayed in the guest room once when he came to inspect the Bushmann apartment as a possible place to settle when they first learned that their building was going to be demolished. He had planned to return at a later date to inspect the Di Napoli apartment. But then, after a fire that destroyed a good part of the old building, they had to leave immediately.

The O'Tooles had been extremely helpful, cutting the door into the Di Napoli apartment, aiding them in their move and providing food and shelter when they arrived.

After a long, tedious descent through seven more levels, Zort and Krim reached the basement. Here they had to lower a rope ladder since they were leaving the wall space and entering the large boiler room. Zort climbed down a few rungs of the ladder and looked around. A dim light cast ragged shadows of a complex of pipes, tanks and boilers. The hum of a large motor and the roar of a powerful oil burner flame made the room sound like a factory. At this hour of the morning there was never anyone in the boiler room.

"It's all clear, Krim. Let's go." Zort hurried down to the floor, followed by his nephew.

"This way," instructed Zort.

"You sure that's the way to the oil tank?" asked Krim.

"Perfectly sure."

They walked along a row of odd-shaped valves and gauges, past the huge oil burner, with its little window glowing bright orange from the fire, and past three small, odd-shaped tanks. Finally, they arrived at their destination: a fifteen-hundred-gallon oil storage tank.

"Come on," said Zort. "It's on the other side of the tank, against the wall."

"It sure is a safe place to store things. The big people could never get anywhere near it," observed Krim.

The two little people scampered across the six-inch space below the tank. It got darker, but there was still enough light for them to see. Soon they reached the back wall.

"Here it is. Just where we left it." They were looking at what appeared to be a large flattened box painted in a manner as to make it look shabby. In fact, it was made of sturdy sheets of plastic and was thoroughly weatherproof.

"Grab that end. We've got to pull it outside, where we can assemble it."

Zort and Krim dragged the structure across the floor to the basement door. With a spring, Zort jumped to the doorknob. Then he let down a rope to which Krim tied a special tool. Zort inserted the tool into the keyhole, maneuvered it for a few minutes, then click, the door was unlocked.

A few minutes later the two little men used another tool to pry open the huge basement door. A chilly fresh breeze swept into the musty room.

"Let's get this outside quickly. Ya never know when someone will come along."

It was a dark, cloudy night with a stiff late autumn breeze and a smell of rain in the air. Bits of paper and dried leaves whirled around, beating against brick walls and settling into wind-free corners. The only light that entered the alleyway was strands and fragments of lamppost light that reflected off the windows of a building across the street. But the deep black shadows were always a comfort to Wall People.

The threat of rain was welcome to them. In fact, they always made their journeys at night and preferably during a rainstorm or in the winter when the cold, dreary weather kept late-night pedestrians off the street. Zort and Krim worked with great speed. By pushing firmly against the sides of the container, they caused it to open into a rectangular box, six inches high, eight inches wide and a foot long.

Next, they attached a set of wheels, which enabled them to push the box like a wagon. This was their moving van, into which they would place the rest of their household belongings for transport from the old house.

Zort and Krim were easily able to push the van up the alleyway ramp to the large iron gate at street level. These ramps, which are found on the sides of many large buildings in New York, are used by the big people for delivery of large cartons and furniture into the service entrance. Once again, through the use of their special tools, the gate was unlocked and opened. Zort poked his head out and looked east and west on 85th Street. At 1:30 a.m. it was deserted.

"It's all clear. Let's go."

They made good speed toward Park Avenue. At the corner, they stopped, staying close to the building. Once again Zort checked the area, carefully looking around the corner to Park Avenue. He could see the awning at the main entrance to their building. The doorman was obviously inside.

They were about to turn the corner when they were flooded in light. A car with its brights on was coming down the street. With unbelievable speed, Zort and Krim darted through a door in the back of their moving van. As the car drove by, all that could be seen was what appeared to be a dirty old carton on the sidewalk. Inside the van, Zort and Krim could hear the car come to a stop. Had the driver seen them? Would he get out and come over to the box?

"Maybe we should get out of here," whispered Krim.

"Shh. I'm listening. He hasn't opened the car door yet."

A moment later the car roared away.

"I guess he just stopped for light," said Krim.

Zort rubbed his bony chin. "Sure now, I can feel it in these old bones, 'tis not going to be an easy trip."

The men got out and pushed the van around the corner, then raced past the building entrance and up the block toward 86th Street. There they would have to be extremely careful. It was a wide street to cross, with bus and car traffic even at this hour.

Zort checked. The marquee of the movie theaters and the store windows were all dark. The crowds that normally mill along 86th Street, looking at bookstore windows and entering restaurants, were long gone. He turned to Krim. "Don't forget. We move the van to the curb and quickly lower it to the gutter. As soon as it's clear of traffic, race across the street with all the speed possible."

"I know, Uncle Zort. We've done this kind of a thing a half-dozen times before," Krim said with a trace of nervousness in his voice.

"Yes. But I've done it a hundred times. So you're still new at it. Let's go."

The crossing went smoothly to Krim's great relief. The next block was fairly dark, which would make things easier for them. But the wind was acting up, making it difficult to control the van. It was like trying to hold onto a large kite.

All was going well when it happened. A powerful gust of wind sent the empty van spinning and tumbling up the street. Zort and Krim held on for dear life, unable to control the flight of the van. They were battered, scraped, bruised and dragged. But they did not let go. Then, as suddenly as it had started, the wind died down, leaving the box on its side against a building. Krim got up. He was badly bruised, and he ached all over, but was not seriously hurt.

"Get this thing off me," came a voice from below the van. Krim grabbed the side of the box and lifted.

"Are you okay, Uncle Zort?"

The patriarch raised himself up and flexed his arms and legs, he picked up his hat from the ground and pressed it securely on his head. "Nothing broken, I guess. But 'tis better we get moving. That was just the beginning. Sure now, we're going to get hit by a whopper of a storm."

With this new threat in mind, they continued their trip at an even faster pace. They crossed 87th Street with no problems and approached 88th Street, unaware that they had been spotted by an unleashed Doberman pinscher.

Just in the nick of time, Zort's sense of danger was aroused. He looked back. The dog was nearly upon them, charging like a gigantic monster bent on devouring his prey in a single vicious motion of its powerful jaws. "Quick. In the van," he warned, pushing his nephew through the door and leaping in behind him. The barking and growling told them that the beast was upon them. The van shook violently as the dog sunk his fangs into it.

"What'll we do, Uncle Zort? He'll kill us. We don't stand a chance."

Zort reached into the bag of tools. "Courage lad. Take this. If he sticks his head in, jab the beast in the soft part of his nose."

It'll never stop him. We're as good as dead," said Krim, nearly panicked as the van was tumbled and shaken in the jaws of the dog.

Zort did not answer. He just waited with a sharp tool in his hands ready to fight for his life the moment the dog broke through.

Then they heard the voice of a man. "Sampson! Sampson! Stop it. Come here, Sampson."

The voice got closer. "Get over here, you crazy dog. Get away from the filthy old box." There was the clicking sound of a chain. "Okay, let's go, Sampson. You've been out long enough."

The voice was moving away.

Neither Zort nor Krim moved for a while, their hands still trembling with fright. After five minutes of silence, they emerged from the van. Surprisingly, it had not been as badly damagd as they had imagined.

"Sure now, 'tis a sturdy vehicle we've built," said Zort, with a sense of relief.

Finally, they reached 89th Street. Zort and Krim pushed the van around the corner to the iron gate that led to the courtyard. They had no trouble unlocking it or the back door to the basement. But just as they entered the old place, the wind began to gust again and a light rain started falling. In the distance, they heard the ominous rumble of thunder, reminding them that the return trip might be far more perilous.

"Light the lamp. I can't see a thing," said Zort.

"It sure is damp down here," observed Krim. "I wish we had a vapor bowl for protection," he added, holding the lamp up and looking around the deserted basement.

"We can't worry about that now. We've got to move quickly. Just keep your eyes wide open."

They walked over to where the stairway to the upper floors was located. Krim swung a rope with a metal hook and cast it up to the ceiling. It caught. He quickly climbed up and dropped a ladder. Then he returned to the floor to help carry up the tools. They were about to ascend the ladder when Zort made a motion for them to freeze. He had spotted something across the room.

A rat.

With a blood curdling squeal, beady red eyes glowing, the beast lunged across the basement floor. Zort quickly reached into his pocket and threw something at the attacker. There was a puff of smoke, and a very familiar odor. The rat stopped short, hesitated for a moment, then turned and fled.

Krim sniffed. "That's from the vapor bowls. How'd you do that?"

"I knew we'd need something like that for this trip, so I conjoured up a Zort special, these little balls of vapor bowl powder."

"They'll sure come in handy," said Krim.

"Blow out the lantern," directed Zort. "The light will just attract a lot of unwanted guests. We can make it up the ladder in the dark."

The two Wall People began the long climb to their old home on the eleventh floor. It was pitch dark. Krim's imagination ran wild with thoughts of terrifying predators closing in on them from all sides. Time seemed to stand still; a minute seemed like an hour. Yet nothing happened as they climbed in silence for about ten minutes, with Zort leading the way.

On the fifth floor Krim stopped for a moment to catch his breath. He marveled at his old uncle's ability to keep up such a steady pace. That's when he heard Zort complaining.

"What on earth!" What's this?"

Silence followed. Krim began to climb quickly to catch up with Zort.

"Krim! Get up here fast. I'm stuck in something."

Krim quickly lit the lamp and held it above his head. He couldn't believe his eyes. His uncle was completely entwined in a spider's web. Thick strands were wound around his head, arms and chest. But far more terrible, just above Zort was a huge spider, measuring a full three inches across, making its way down to its entrapped victim. In all his years Krim had never seen such a large spider. He knew that he must act immediately.

"Don't move, Uncle. I'm coming." Krim reached into his bag, took out a large needle and managed to climb around his uncle, placing himself between Zort and the spider.

The beast dropped with terrible speed. Krim gripped the ladder tightly with one arm and held the needle before him. The battle was on. The legs of the spider moved in all directions, threatening to entrap Krim. Krim jabbed the needle into his adversary over and over again. But the spider kept coming. Finally, in one desperate effort, Krim lunged forward and plunged the miniature spear deep into the spider's underside. The beast made a convulsive shudder and flopped over. Krim took a long deep breath, wiped the sweat from his brow and looked down at his uncle.

"Splendid fight, lad, splendid fight. Couldn't have done better myself," said Zort proudly. "Now kindly help me out of this tangle."

A few minutes later, he was free, and they continued their climb . . . with the lantern lit. Finally, they reached the old apartment, a beautiful accommodation, by Wall People's standards.

It was a series of little rooms, brightly painted in a rainbow of colors. The kitchen, which was also the family room, was painted bright yellow, with beautiful murals of Irish scenery decorating the walls. Individual bedrooms were pink, blue, green and even orange.

"Let's get the stove down first," said Zort. The two men worked at a feverish pace, disconnecting the stove and dismantling it into smaller pieces. It took about an hour to get everything down to the basement. Just before-starting down with the last load, Krim and Zort paused for a moment, casting a final gaze at their old home.

"It certainly holds a lot of memories." Krim sighed.

" 'Tis a lifetime of livin'—happiness, sadness, deaths, births, celebrations, mourning— sure now, more memories than one soul can recall, alive in these rooms, locked in the hearts of these walls," Zort added plaintively.

"Remember the day I met Alba for the first time?"

"Do I remember, lad? Brack O'Regan and I nearly split a gut laughin'. Brack and Peggy had brought their daughter up for the first time, pretendin' they were making an ordinary social call, when all the time Mrs. O'Regan had her eye on fetchin' you for her daughter."

Krim's face broke into a broad smile. "And there I was, all sweaty and dirty from working on the kitchen stove when they walked in unannounced."

"I'll never forget how furious you were. Here's this pretty little young lady, carrying a huge bowl of pudding as a gift . . . your tools scattered around the floor and you on your hands and knees. She trips over a tool; the bowl goes flying and lands on your head. You get up, filthy as a pig, with puddin' runnin down your chest, a bowl on your head, and Brack and I croakin' with laughter."

"Poor Alba, she was so upset, she ran down to her house, and we didn't meet again for two months."

"So many memories," said Zort. "Things were so much simpler. Living was so much less of a challenge, less traffic, fewer people, more of an opportunity to get out and breathe a little fresh air.

The mood suddenly turned more serious.

"Uncle Zort, what will we do when there are no more old buildings for us to live in?"

"Lad, you're worrying about problems of the distant future. Right now we have other things to worry about . . ."

Just then, a loud clap of thunder rumbled across the sky above the building.

". . . Like getting our belongings home while we can. Let's load the van. We're running out of time."

An hour later they had finished tying everything down securely. Zort looked at Krim. "Ready?"

"Ready as I'll ever be, Uncle."

"Then let's get going."

They inserted the tool to open the basement door. As they unlatched it, the door went flying open with a crash from the force of the wind. Zort and Krim looked out with shock.

"Holy mackerel," said Krim. "Look at that rain. I've never seen it come down so heavy."

A torrent of water was falling, causing veritable rivers to flow along the ground. Little lakes formed in depressions, the water swirling from the wind. Strong gusts caused sheets of rain to violently swirl sideways, smashing against anything or anyone in its path. The only sound louder than the beating rain was the crashing of thunder following streaks of lightning that lit the area like the noonday sun.

Krim had to shout to be heard. "What are we goin to do? We can't go out in that storm!"

"We've got to," answered Zort with authority.

"But we'll be drowned. Look at it, even the big people would have trouble walking through the storm. We won't make it a block."

"We'll have to take our chances," insisted the patriarch.

"We don't have a chance. The only thing is to stay here until the storm dies down."

Zort got close to his nephew and looked at him sternly. A flash of lightning lit the area, revealing eyes blazing with determination. "Krim! Take hold of yourself. We've been in tougher situations than this. We have no choice, don't you see. The wreckers will be coming tomorrow to tear down this building, so we can't stay through tomorrow. And if we wait too much longer, it will be daylight before we get home. We're flirting with death either way. So we've got to leave right now. You've got to trust my judgment."

Krim looked out as a flash of lightning revealed a world of wind and swirling waters. It would take no less than a miracle to make it back. Then he looked at his uncle. "Okay, Uncle Zort. I've always trusted your judgment. I won't stop now. Let's go."

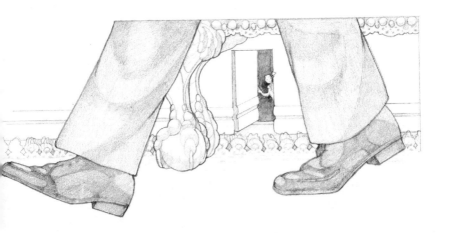

5 * Break-In

At 3:15 a.m., not a minute before or a minute after, but precisely 3:15, Black Jack appeared in the dark doorway where he had stood earlier that evening. Precision and thoroughness were his hallmarks. Everything he did was planned to a degree of exactness that would do justice to a great scientific project. His every movement was methodical and carefully measured.

For a full fifteen minutes he stood in the doorway, motionless, his eyes searching, like a hawk scanning his domain for prey. His mind could almost measure the degree of blackness of the night. But the blackness was shattered every few minutes as jagged rods of lightning accentuated the raging storm.

At 3:30, Black Jack crossed Park Avenue and glided like a shadow along 85th Street to the service alleyway behind the large apartment building in which the Di Napoli family lived. He planned to unlock the large wrought iron gate and enter the building through the basement door. He had developed his trade as a burglar to a point of near perfection, and ordinary locks were like toys to him.

Jack paused for a moment and looked around to be sure there were no witnesses. The violence of the storm guaranteed that no one would venture out except in an extreme emergency. The roar of the wind as it shook the trees provided added cover for any noise made during his forced entry. Jack glanced across the street, the dark brown four-door sedan was waiting. And although he could not see him, Jack knew that Zero was in the car, lying down so that the car would appear empty to a possible passerby. Zero never failed to do as he was told.

Jack examined the gate for a few seconds, then took a ring of lock picks from his pocket and slipped a large pick into the lock. To his surprise, even before he turned the pick, when he pushed on the gate, it swung open. He whipped around and stared intently up and down the street.

It's a trap! he thought. *Why would the gate be open at this hour?* For several minutes Black Jack remained motionless, his eyes straining to spot anything suspicious. Finally, he decided that the gate had been left unlocked by a careless worker. Maybe Zero had seen someone leave. He decided to check.

As he approached the car, Jack could see no one in it. Was it possible that Zero was not there? If so, it would be the first time he had failed Jack.

However, upon arriving at the car he could see something heaped on the front seat covered by a black blanket. Jack tapped on the window. Nothing happened. He tapped a little louder, and the blanket moved, revealing Zero's bald head. Jack motioned for Zero to lower the window.

"What's wrong, boss? Wasn't I hidin' good enough? I didn't move . . . even a little . . . even when the lightin' and tunder was all crazy."

"Be quiet fool. I just want to know if you've seen anyone leave the back entrance of the building."

"Nothing . . . . I seen nothing" insisted Zero. "Like I says, I stayed outta sight. Just like you said to do. So I seen nothing."

"Okay. I was just checking."

Jack looked at his watch. "It's twenty to four. I'll be down in exactly one hour. At four thirty, go through the gate and wait for me in the basement. You can help me get everything into the car. Is that clear?"

"Ya boss, poifectly clear."

Black Jack returned to the building. His bony hand gripped the gate and pushed it open just enough to slip through. Once in the court-yard, he walked quickly down the ramp to the doorway that led into the basement of the building. Out came the lock picks again. But the pick was not necessary. The door was unlocked. It swung open with a slight screech. Black Jack froze. He flattened himself against the wall, not daring to breathe.

"Surely a trap," he concluded. "First the gate, now the door. Too suspicious." He looked to his left. There was a ten-foot-high stone wall, topped by a six-foot chain link fence. It divided the apartment backyard from the backyards of the brownstones along 85th Street. To his right was the long ramp to the iron gate; the only route of escape.

Who could possibly know about my plan, he thought.

"No one," was his answer. "No one, that is, except Zero," he muttered crossly. If that dumb ox made a slip about this job, it'll be the last one he ever makes."

A few minutes of silence convinced him that he was safe for the present. If anyone wanted to capture him, now would have been the time. But perhaps they were waiting for him inside?

The intruder pushed the basement door open a little more. All was silent. Like a soldier in battle, his eyes searched the room. Everything was suspect. Someone could be hiding behind the huge boiler, the large brick columns or the machinery.

Jack took a breath, stepped inside . . . and waited, ready to react at any moment to the slightest action. The humming of the oil gun and the low roar of the powerful flame in the boiler were the only sounds that met his sensitive ears between the thunderclaps and the gusts of wind. He had to make a quick decision. Either turn and run, and waste weeks of preparation, or proceed with all haste.

Greed won out, and without hesitation, Black Jack closed the door and threaded his way around the machinery to the inner door, which led to the lobby. He was greatly relieved to find it locked. It indicated that there was less likelihood that a trap had been set. He quickly picked the lock. Very carefully, he opened the door . . . The lobby was well lit. At the center of the lobby was a richly polished cherrywood mail desk, which matched small tables and finely upholstered couches.

Unfortunately for Black Jack, the doorman was standing at the mail desk, in full view of the basement door. Normally he should be standing at the front door. There was nothing left to do but curse his bad luck. For a moment Jack thought of charging out and killing the doorman. But suddenly he heard a voice. Someone was calling into the lobby.

"Hey, Mike." It was the doorman from next door.

"What is it, Henry?"

"I bought you a cup of coffee. It'll hit the spot at this hour."

The man at the mail desk walked out of the lobby to the front entrance.

Black Jack didn't waste a second. He rushed from the basement door, silently stole across the lobby and entered the main stairway leading to the upper floors. There was no stopping him now. Next stop, the Di Napoli apartment.

A sense of excitement gripped him as he opened the door on the fourteenth floor and peeked into the richly carpeted hallway. All was quiet. He poked his head through the doorway. He looked right, then left. Not a soul in sight.

Black Jack picked up his bag and walked along the hallway until he came to apartment 14G. The door was secured with two locks.

Picking them turned out to be more of a problem than he had expected. But finally, a soft click told him that he had succeeded. The door swung open.

Black Jack stepped in stood there for a few minutes, reading the vibrations in the air for any indication that someone might be up and around and allowing his eyes to get used to the darkness. Then slowly, with measured steps, he made his way through the foyer and into the living room.

With the aid of a flashlight, he quickly surveyed the room. The information he had gathered, and paid well for, so far had all been correct. There, in the corner, was the china closet that held part of Mrs. Di Napoli's fine porcelain collection. The other valuables were located in the dining room.

Next he took out a slice of fresh steak doused with knockout drops. He moved his flashlight until it settled on the huge shaggy dog lying in the corner, under the piano. The dog, whose head was cocked to one side, studied Black Jack curiously, not quite sure how to react.

Quickly Jack tossed the steak to the dog, who sniffed at it for a moment and then began to devour it with great energy.

That'll keep you asleep for a few hours, thought Jack. *Now to go to work*. He proceeded to the china closet. The finely polished piece of furniture was itself a collector's item. But its contents were Jack's target.

A quick twist of one of his lock picks opened the curved glass door. Jack reached in and inspected some of the porcelains. First he picked up a beautiful bowl and cover, about six inches in diameter, decorated with delicate pastoral scenes and finished in gold trim. He turned it over; there was a mark: crossed swords and the number 2 in gold. "Meissen, and very old" he whispered. "Worth a couple of thousand."

Black Jack reached into his bag, took out a sheet of foam rubber and wrapped the valuable bowl with great care. Then he continued to inspect the other items. He rejected the Wedgwood jasper plaques. They were worth only four or five hundred dollars each. *Only the best for Black Jack* he thought.

Finally, he took a green porcelain vase, made in Paris about 1740; a beautiful cameo vase and a collection of valuable enamel miniatures. He worked swiftly, but with a dexterity that would do justice to a brain surgeon; the entire operation took less than twenty minutes.

He felt a sense of satisfaction as he picked up the bag and headed for the dining room. Just the items from the china closet would make the night's work profitable. Next came the safe. That's where he'd make his real haul. His well-paid information sources told him that Mrs. Di Napoli owned three or four large diamond rings, an expensive pearl necklace and other jewelry of high value. They were kept along with a nice bundle of cash, in the safe.

Black Jack pushed open the dining room door and directed his light around the room. "Some swanky joint," he murmured softly. He quickly walked around the dining room table to the sideboard, ignoring the fine collection of silverware. He put down his bag, reached up and lifted a beautiful still-life painting from its hook. What was revealed seemed to be merely a finely crafted wood-paneled wall. But Jack knew better. He pressed a piece of molding, and one of the small panels slid to the side. There it was, the Di Napoli safe, just waiting to be opened. The operation required absolute silence so he could hear the tumblers fall. The storm outside did not help matters. He had to stop his work with each clap of thunder. He leaned forward and was about to start when he heard it. Very faintly, but unquestionably . . . The sound of footsteps.

A dozen panic-riddled thoughts flashed into his mind. Had it turned out to be a trap after all? Should he run out, leaving everything behind? But he rejected that idea and confidently went into action. Racing around the table, Black Jack hid behind the dining room door, reached into his pocket and took out a razor-sharp switchblade knife.

The sound of the steps got louder. Jack remained motionless, gripping his knife firmly.

The door opened, and someone walked in.

Black Jack sprang like a panther. With lightning-fast motion he wound his arm around the victim's neck, placing the gleaming knife next to his throat. Unfortunately, they were off balance. The attacker and his victim fell with a loud bang against the door.

"Che vuoi! Che vuoi! Aiuto, Aiuto!"

"Shut up, you old fool," threatened Jack. "Speak English, or I'll cut your throat."

"Ama no speak Englisha too good. Please mista, no hurta me."

Just then another voice was heard from the bedroom stairway. "Is that you, Papa? Are you all right?"

Black Jack pulled the old man's face close to his, placed the sharp point of the knife against Nonno's throat and whispered with a snakelike hiss, "Tell her there's nothing wrong! Understand? And tell her to come in here!"

A look of horror gripped Nonno. "No," he pleaded.

"Do it, or I'll go out there and cut her throat."

The old man turned his head and called out with as steady voice as he could. *Non ce male . . . vene qui.*

The sound of steps in the living room quickened, and soon Mrs. Di Napoli entered the room.

For a moment she was confused by the darkness. But she quickly made out the frightening scene.

Instantly Black Jack signaled her not to make a sound. "One scream, and your papa is dead."

"Please, don't hurt him. He's an old man."

"Nobody'll get hurt if you just cooperate."

"What do you want? Whatever it is, take it and leave," she pleaded in a quivering voice.

"To start off with, stay nice and quiet while I tie up Pop here."

Mrs. Di Napoli could barely contain her anguish as Black Jack reached into his bag, took some nylon cord and tied the old man's hands and feet, forcing him to the floor against the wall.

"Now, it's your turn, dear lady."

Mrs. D. hesitated. She was frozen with fear. All she could think of was the children. Suppose they were to wake up. "Dear God, please let them sleep through this," said Mrs. D. in silent prayer.

Black Jack impatiently reached out, grabbed her wrist and pulled her to him. She let out a faint cry as he twisted her arms behind her and wrapped a cord securely around her wrists, then he pushed her against the wall and forced her to sit on the floor next to Nonno.

She looked up pleadingly, tears streaming from her eyes. "What are you going to do to us?"

"Do to you?" repeated Jack. "Why nothing.

I'm merely going to provide a house cleaning service. Yes! That's it." He chuckled. "I'm going to clean the house."

At that, he returned to the safe. There was very little light, so Mrs. D. could barely see what he was doing. The burglar resumed his work, listening at the safe door while he slowly turned the combination lock knob. The silence was broken every so often by a peal of thunder. The storm seemed to be hampering his progress. As the time passed, Black Jack appeared to become irritable. Something was going wrong.

Mrs. D. tried to remain calm. She knew that, above all, she must not cry out or in any way panic. Yet she knew Black Jack was growing frustrated by the safe. It would not open, and Mrs. D. knew that meant serious trouble.

❄   ❄   ❄

At 3:30 a.m., members of the Calabash clan were all awake: Buttercup and Vand were huddled together on a large pillow in the corner of the main room talking quietly. Grandma was sitting in her rocker, knitting. Starlight was helping her mother fold some large pieces of cloth, and Frollin was sitting on a low stool in silence.

A few minutes later Buttercup ran over to Grandma, her eyes big as saucers. "I just thought of something terrible," she said with a sense of excitement that might accompany a major calamity.

"What is it, little darlin'?" Grandma smiled, reaching out her arm and drawing Buttercup close to her.

"Well . . . we forgot something very important. We forgot to send our new address to Santa Claus. He won't know where to bring our presents."

"Is that what's worrying your dear little head. Well now, didn't I tell you before that Santa is very wise and knows a great deal about people. He has all sorts of ways of knowin' where we are and when we move from one place to another."

"Oh! he must be wonderful," said Buttercup. "But I still don't understand . . ."

Buttercup tilted her head to one side and wrinkled her nose. "Santa is big and round, and he can come down the chimney. But how can he get into the wall spaces to bring us our presents?"

Grandma's smile softened, and she became a bit more serious. "He has the spirit of love and Christmas joy, and mere walls can't keep the spirit of Christmas out of anyplace where there is love."

"Why aren't they back, Mother? Daddy and Uncle Zort should have been back by now," Starlight suddenly cried out.

"Now don't start getting upset. It's only

been two hours since they left. I'm sure they'll be back any moment now. They're two grown men, with a lot of experience in the outside world," said Alba.

Silence followed, broken by furious claps of thunder.

"Maybe it took longer than expected to get the furniture down to the basement."

Once again silence.

"Maybe . . ." Alba's voice trailed off awkwardly. She looked at Grandma. Any one of a thousand things could have happened: a stray dog, a cat, automobiles, people and a bad storm, such as the one that was raging right now, were all causes for alarm.

Grandma read the worried look on Alba's face. "There, there, now, darlin'. Don't be creatin' problems where there's none. They'll be fine, those two."

Grandma was quiet for a few minutes, deep in thought. Then she raised her head again. "If you're thinkin' what Zort and Krim are doin' is dangerous, you should think about your unfortunate ancestors who lived in the old country when they had just become small."

Grandma, who now had Buttercup on her lap, motioned for Alba and Starlight to sit next to her. "While we're waitin', let me tell you about those poor souls."

The old woman paused for a moment, to gather her thoughts. "For about two hundred years, the little people managed to survive in the protection of the rugged mountains known as the Twelve Bens. It wasn't easy. As the poor souls got smaller, many of them fell prey to local animals."

"Were there ferocious beasts, or mountain lions around?" asked Starlight.

"No. But there were red foxes, pine martens, minks, otters and badgers. Because of the small size of the people, these animals were a very serious threat. Many a brave lad or unsuspecting mother or child was killed by these animals."

"That must have been horrible," said Buttercup.

"It was indeed," agreed Grandma. "Eventually, some of the little people decided that it might be safer to live within the protection of a large building. Now there were those who did not agree. It was safer in the mountains, they claimed. They had established themselves in a series of small caves. With fires going constantly, wild animals would not enter. Besides, the only place where they could live without being discovered was the great castle of Tara, near Dublin. That would require a journey of a hundred and fifty miles. The clan, many felt, could never make it, not with wild beasts, large rivers and mountains to cross and the big people to evade. Such a trip would mean certain death for the entire four hundred souls in the clan.

"But others argued differently. A month did not go by without one of the clan being killed by an animal. Remaining in the mountains simply meant the slow death of the clan. If they lived at Tara, they would be safe from wild animals and could always get food from the large storerooms. Besides, they had been completely out of touch with civilization and were losing their own sense of humanity. There was more to being a human being than just survival. They craved to know what was going on in literature, medicine, politics.

"After many weeks of discussion, the argument was finally resolved. A group of ten families, fifty souls in all, would make the journey. If they survived the trip and were able to maintain themselves at the castle for two years, they would send for the others."

"That must have been a terribly exciting journey!" exclaimed Starlight.

"That it was, darlin'," answered Grandma. "They almost did not reach Tara, what with the strong current of the Shannon, storms, near starvation and wild beasts. More than half the group perished on the way. But under the leadership of a brave young man named John Creedon, they reached the grand castle and started a new life."

"Oh, please tell us about that journey," pleaded Buttercup.

Alba suddenly stood up. "Something is terribly wrong. Listen to that storm. Lord knows what's happened to Krim and Uncle Zort."

She turned to Frollin. He understood immediately and got up. Alba placed a hand on his shoulder, her eyes moist. "Go down to the basement and look for your father and Uncle Zort. They may need help."

Frollin gave his mother a gentle hug, then turned and quietly left the room. A small lamp lighted his way as he descended the long narrow ladder that led fourteen stories.

The boy's eyes darted right and left as his lantern created sinister shadows on the rough walls. One thought persisted in his mind: outside of the living area he did not have the protection of the vapor bowls. Every moving black shadow seemed to hide a deadly predator. Instinctively, Frollin glanced down at the knife on his belt.

Even moving at a very fast pace, it took over twenty minutes to reach the basement. From the last rung of the ladder he could glance into the giant room. There he remained, silent and listening.

The room was filled with the roar of the boiler, interrupted by the shattering sounds of the storm. His eyes darted from machine to machine. But there was no trace of Krim or Zort.

He waited ten minutes. There was not the slightest indication that anyone was in the basement. The storm made it sound as though a great battle was raging outside. Claps of thunder seemed to shake the very foundations of the building. As his eyes darted around the room, Frollin spotted something climbing up the wall straight toward him. He strained to make out what it was. Then it came out of the dark shadows, a large water bug, perhaps two inches long.

In the wall spaces, large waterbugs were considered extremely vicious. Their hook-shaped legs could latch onto prey, trapping a victim in a death grip. They were frightening and utterly repulsive creatures. Frollin knew that he shouldn't run. If he tried to and fell, the creature might be aroused to attack, perhaps flying up and leaping on his back.

Frollin's heart pounded, and his hands began to shake with terror. He felt terribly alone and helpless. But he swallowed hard, gripped his knife and waited without moving a muscle. Up the wall crawled the hideous-looking creature. Frollin decided that he would strike a quick blow with his knife, hoping to send the ghastly thing falling to the basement floor.

But what if the water bug were to begin to fly? What could he do then? The next minute felt like an eternity, as the creature came ever closer.

Fear made it look twice its size. Frollin thought his heart would burst with fright.

Then, in an unexpected move, and to Frollin's great relief, the water bug suddenly changed its path and crawled off in another direction. The boy waited a few minutes, then decided to return to the house. Father and Uncle Zort were certainly not in the basement.

The near encounter with the water bug and the thought that his father and uncle were possibly in a desperate situation seemed to drain all the life out of his body. He dragged himself up the fourteenth floor, but hesitated at the entrance to the Big People's apartment. He had strict orders never to go near there. "There will be time enough for such adventures when you are older," warned his father.

Yet he held up his lantern and looked at the miniature doorway. It was locked, so they could not be in there. He turned and was about to continue up the ladder when he heard a woman's cry.

Without a second thought, he unlatched the door, opened it a crack and listened. It was quiet. But Frollin had a feeling that something was terrible wrong in the Di Napoli apartment. So he made a rash decision and entered the world of the Big People.

❄   ❄   ❄

Even with the meager illumination of a flashlight, the expression of rage and frustration on
Black Jack's face was obvious. He could not understand it. His nimble, sensitive fingers had
failed him. After a dozen tries, the safe was still
locked. Part of the problem was that wretched
storm with its infernal thunder, he concluded.
But he still should have been able to open this
simple safe.

Or was it so simple? Maybe there was something that he had not learned about the safe.
Like a trick or a second lock. The rogue stood
silently, pondering the problem. Then he walked
around the table and bent over Mrs. Di Napoli.

"I want you to be a nice girl and open the
safe. That's simple enough, isn't it" asked Jack.

"I can't. I don't know the combination."

"You're lying." he hissed, his eyes ablaze
with anger. "You must have the combination."

"No, no. You've got to believe me; I don't,"
she pleaded.

Black Jack read her face. "Oh, of course, Mr.
D. has the combination."

In one cruel, rough move, he grabbed her
arm, lifted her up and half dragged her to the
dining room door. "Okay! Listen to me carefully
if you know what's good for you. Call Mr. D. and
tell him to come down here. No tricks, do ya
hear?"

Utter panic gripped her. "I can't. It'll wake up the whole house. Besides, he'll know something is wrong."

"Ya better think fast, or I'll go up there and get him myself," he threatened.

The very thought of such a vile character going upstairs where the children were sleeping nearly made her faint. "All right," she said. "Only you'd better turn on the dining room light. He knows I would not stay down here in the dark."

Black Jack reached over and turned on the lights, revealing himself to her for the first time. "Make it good now," he warned. "I'll be right behind this door. Anything goes wrong . . . you and Pops get it first."

"John . . . John," trying to call just loud enough for him to hear but not enough to wake the children.

Silence followed.

"John . . . John."

More silence.

Then there was a hushed voice from the balcony. "What do you want, Mary? Is something wrong.

There was a momentary silence as Mrs. Di Napoli's mind desperately searched for an answer. "Yes," she said. "It's Dad. He tripped and sprained his ankle. I need to get him upstairs."

As John Di Napoli walked into the dining room, a glance told him the real story, and the color drained from his face. "Oh my God," he uttered.

Black Jack's knife was at Mary's throat. There was no question but that the burglar would not hesitate to kill her. "Don't try to be a big hero, Mr. D., or your pretty little wife becomes a has-been," warned the burglar.

"Now take it easy, Mac," said John. "Just tell me what it is you want."

"The first thing is for you to turn around, stand against the wall and put your hands behind your back."

John followed instructions. A few minutes later, his hands and feet were securely tied.

"Okay, Mr. D., it's really simple. All you have to do is tell me how to open the safe, and I'll be on my way."

"First, you let my wife and my father-in-law go, then I'll give what you want," answered John.

"Hey! will you listen to macho man. All tied up and still bargaining," Black Jack said with a smile on his face. "Here's a better deal. If you don't tell me how to open the safe in one minute, I'll start carving up the lady of the house. How do you like them apples?"

"All right. First you've got to go to the picture at the end of the room and push it to the right. Now press the brass plate in and upward, and you'll see a series of five buttons."

"I see them," said Jack. "Now what?"

"Press the second button three times. The fourth button once and the fifth button twice."

A soft buzzing tone sounded as Jack finished pressing the fifth button, and a small red light glowed at the safe panel. "Now the safe will open with the normal combination: right to seven, left past seven to eleven, then right to eighteen." Black Jack turned the knob to the combination numbers and turned a handle that unlocked the door. As the safe swung open, the villain turned to his victims, a wicked smile crossed his lips.

"Now, that's more like it."

The flashlight beam was swallowed up by the safe as Jack reached in and cleaned out its contents. First, he examined a flat velvet-colored jewel box. He snapped it open and spotlighted its contents. Shimmering in the light was a bracelet of alternate rows of small rubies and diamonds. "This alone is worth the job," he murmured.

Next he examined a pear-shaped diamond ring and a sapphire and diamond cluster ring. He looked across the room. "Hey, lady, you sure married a big spender."

There was also a pack of bills, mostly twenties and fifties, other assorted jewelry and a lot of documents, mostly stocks and bonds in the safe. Jack placed the jewelry and cash into his bag.

"Okay, you've got what you want, now get out," insisted Mr. Di Napoli.

Black Jack's eyes narrowed as he walked across the room and spoke softly and clearly. "First of all, big spender, I'm not ready to leave. There's still some more cleaning up I want to do."

Then Jack pressed his face close to his victims and hissed the next words. "Second . . . before I leave, I'm gonna kill all three of you."

No one was aware of Frollin, standing behind the partially opened door, watching the scene intently.

6 ✳ A Stormy Return

Within seconds of stepping out of the basement, Zort and Krim were soaking wet. And the wind, which whipped the rain violently in all directions, made it difficult to breathe.

"You push, and I'll pull," instructed Zort.

"What did you say?" shouted Krim.

Zort cupped his hands around his mouth and repeated. "You push and I'll pull."

Krim nodded.

The fully loaded cart was heavy to start with. But the flowing water made it even more difficult to move the vehicle. It took all their strength to get it rolling. Slowly they inched their way toward the ramp that led to the street level. Little by little the vehicle picked up speed. The howling wind, beating rain, flashing lightning and exploding thunder were terrifying. The only benefit of these conditions, thought Zort, was that not a living soul would be fool enough to be out on the street.

When they finally reached the ramp, the momentum of the van carried it a way uphill. But then it slowed down, came to a halt and, in spite of their efforts, began to roll down again, coming to a full stop at level ground. Zort walked around to the back of the cart and put his face close to Krim's so he could be heard. "I can't get a good grip up front. We'll have to push together from the back. It'll be easier."

Krim agreed. Both men put their shoulders to the cart and took a deep breath. A sudden lightning flash lit the old building. Zort glanced up, and a dozen memories surged through his mind. Goodbye old house, you've been good to us." Zort sighed to himself.

"Push! Uncle Zort. Push harder," urged Krim.

Zort and Krim tried desperately to get a good grip with their feet. They pushed with all their might; for a few moments it felt as though the cart was glued to the ground, then it began to move. Little by little they advanced uphill. At one instant the wind would be at their backs, aiding them in moving the cart. Then, in a rapid change, it would become a headwind, causing them to nearly lose control of the cart.

"This is crazy, Uncle Zort," shouted Krim, barely audible over the howl of the storm. "We'll never make it to the top."

"Keep pushing. Keep pushing, nephew" encouraged Zort. "We're already halfway there."

The cart continued to inch up, and for a while it appeared that they would make it to the top. Then, suddenly, a furious gust of wind made the burden unbearably heavy. In spite of their heroic effort, the cart began to roll backwards. It picked up speed. Zort and Krim lost their balance, tumbled to the ground, and the cart rolled speedily down the ramp.

The situation appeared hopeless to Krim, as he lay on the ground deep in a puddle.

"Are you all right?" asked Zort, crawling over to him, bleeding from a bruise on his forehead.

"That depends on what you consider all right. No bones broken. But that's the only good news," answered Krim.

They both stood up and surveyed the damage. The cart had rolled far back into the yard.

But it was undamaged. "We're further back than when we started," complained Krim.

"Don't be discouraged, lad," said Zort. "No effort is ever for nothing. Now let's get started again. This time we'll do it right." Zort reached into the cart and pulled out a long rope and tackle. "Here's what we should have done in the first place."

He and Krim tied the rope around the cart. The wind had now increased in intensity; and something else was happening: the temperature was dropping. It felt a lot colder than it had when they had started out. If it started icing up, they'd really be in trouble.

"First, we'll push the cart to the edge of the ramp. Then, I'll tie the rope and tackle around the iron gate. While you push, I'll pull with the rope. That way the cart won't be able to slide back."

They both put their backs to the cart and rolled it to the ramp. Then Zort, with a huge coil of rope over his shoulder, ran up the ramp, unwinding the line as he went along. Once he had the rope and tackle wound around the gate, he waved to his nephew. One pushed and the other pulled, and slowly the loaded cart inched its way up the ramp.

"We made it! We made it! It's all downhill from here," Krim shouted. His arm went around Zort's shoulder.

"We can cheer later. There's still a long way to go," Zort reminded him, as they swung the iron gate open enough to pass the cart through.

Krim and his uncle looked around carefully. Even in this storm and at this early morning hour someone might be out on the street. But no one was in sight.

Although it was much easier pushing the cart on level ground, the violent wind and the torrential rain made every step treacherous. They were nearly at the corner of 89th Street and Park Avenue when a small branch fell from a tree, narrowly missing the adventurers. Now they came to their first street crossing.

"Look at that, Uncle Zort. It's a river," Krim shouted, pointing to the curb. "We'll be carried off by that current."

"No, we won't," Zort assured him. "Here, help me tie the rope around the cart."

"What good will that do?"

"We'll let the cart in first. It's heavy enough to keep us from being carried away."

They pushed the cart off the sidewalk, firmly gripping the rope. The vehicle settled into the water and remained still.

"Okay, Krim. Let's go. Hold on to the cart. It's our only chance to make it across the street."

They jumped off the curb and found themselves waist-deep in fast-running water. It was cold—numbing cold. The temperature was dropping fast. But there was no time to think about discomfort; precious time was passing.

"Push, Krim. Push for all you're worth."

They inched the cart across the water. Only with their mightiest effort was it kept under control. They were out of the deep water and about to roll the wagon across the street when, for the second time that night, the area was suddenly flooded with light.

"A car. Quick, behind the cart," ordered Zort.

The noise of a speeding automobile filled the air. As the machine roared by, a huge wave— a mountain of water—came crashing down on the two little people, completely submerging them and turning the cart on its side.

Krim struggled. He grasped at the cart and held his breath as he went under. Zort was choking from some water he had swallowed and was not helped any by the blasts of rain beating against his face.

"Are you all right, Uncle Zort?"

Zort could not answer for a moment. Finally he got up and rested himself on the overturned cart. He cleared his throat and assured Krim he was okay. After straining and tugging they lifted the cart and pushed it across the street.

Again they entered a swift-flowing river that raged along the curb. On this side the water was chest high. Only the heat generated from hard work kept the two men from freezing in the cold water. The curb towered above them menacingly. So they moved the cart downstream to the corner.

Here it was much easier to get the cart up on the sidewalk because it slanted like a ramp into the street. Using a rope coiled around a near-by letterbox, they pulled their burden to the sidewalk.

With determination and an incredible amount of energy, the two members of the Cala-bash Clan managed to manipulate their vehicle past 88th Street, and 87th Street. There was no letup in the storm. If anything, it seemed to be getting worse.

As they pushed the cart towards 86th Street, violent, jagged bolts of lightning streaked across the black sky. The howling wind whipped sheets of rain across the avenue, sending twist-ing and swirling columns of water smashing against buildings, trees and the little people. But still they kept pushing the cart.

They were halfway down the block when tragedy struck. A fierce blast of wind blew the cart out of control. Zort and Krim, hanging on for dear life, their muscles aching from the strain, were blown to the edge of the curb. There was a blinding lightning flash and a crash as a giant tree branch came plunging down. Suddenly they were in the water—Zort, Krim and the cart. Zort floundered; he went under with great force, as though sucked down by a powerful whirlpool. All was black. The sounds of the storm were muffled and far off. He felt himself pinned by something hard: the cart or the tree branch. If he didn't free himself soon, he would drown. With a purely instinctive reaction, Zort closed his eyes, squeezed his face tightly and summoned every ounce of psychic power. There was no certainty about this power. He was never sure that it would work. But an instant later he was free and floating to the surface.

Once on top of the water he could see that the cart was jammed against the fallen tree branch.

His first thought was of his nephew. "Krim, Krim . . . where are you?"

No answer.

Zort looked in all directions. No sign of Krim. He called out to his nephew again, this time louder. Still no answer. Finally he dove beneath the water, thinking that Krim might be pinned by the cart or branch. But feeling around in the freezing black water, he found nothing but hard surfaces. Not a trace of his nephew. He dove several times before admitting that the young man was not in the immediate area.

Then it occured to him that Krim might have been carried away by the swift current. *Lord knows where the waters will take him,* thought Zort. *Oh, saints in heaven, watch over the poor lad.*

Without a moment's hesitation he climbed up onto the cart, leaped to the sidewalk and began running along the curb toward 86th Street. As he ran, Zort kept his eyes peeled on the raging waters, and he called Krim's name over and over, realizing that he was taking a terrible chance, running out in the open so recklessly.

As he passed each parked car along the street, he leaned over and shouted his nephew's name. But all he could hear was the gurgling and splashing of the rushing water, the howling wind and the sound of torrential rain beating against the cars.

"Krim, Krim . . . dear nephew, where are you? Call out if you can hear me," pleaded Zort.

Nearly in a state of panic, he continued running along the edge of the sidewalk and calling Krim's name. He was almost to the corner when he saw a sight that made his heart sink with terror. At this point the rushing water entered what seemed to be a small lake. However, the waters of the lake were swirling in a frightning circle, forming a large whirlpool whose center dropped in a tight funnel into the black yawning mouth of a sewer. With a roar, the river poured into the black subterranean world, flooded with murky water and inhabited by vile, ferocious creatures.

Even if Krim could have survived the fall into the terrible pit, one encounter with a vicious, hungry sewer rat would spell doom for the brave lad, thought Zort.

He stood silent for a while, hypnotized by the violent swirl of the pool. Twigs, leaves and other debris took turns in being trapped in the outer currents then spinning in a frenzy and sinking into the dark world.

"What a horrible way to die. What a sickening, useless way to end such a loving life. And all because of our cursed size. For the big people, this would be an inconvenient puddle. For us 'tis a death trap," he cried out, not caring if anybody heard him.

Tears came to Zort's eyes as he considered his nephew's fate. But he was sure of one thing, Krim had not given up without a struggle. After all, he was a Calabash, so he had courage, character and, above all, a strong will to live. For a few moments, Zort stared at the whirlpool. Suddenly he noticed that, because of an obstruction, part of the sewer was clear of water. He could see into the hole.

"A clear area," he murmured.

Was it possible? Could Krim still be alive down there, with no way to get back up? Zort surveyed the situation. It would be extremely dangerous to go down into the sewer.

"Suppose the obstruction were to move after I got down there?" reasoned Zort. "The spot would be flooded, and I'd be trapped. It would be impossible to make it up through the falling water. Then who would take care of the clan?"

But on the other hand, his nephew might still be alive—down there, all alone, hoping that his great Uncle Zort would come after him. Down there in the dark, cold and frightened. It was a terrible decision to make.

"How could I face Alba? How could I face Krim's children, knowing that I did not even make an attempt to save their father?" Zort agonized.

In an instant the decision was made. He turned and ran up the block to the cart with one strong thought pounding in his head: no one should be judged on what he has accomplished; rather, one should be judged on what he has tried to achieve. Trying was what really counted. If he died, he died; but by all that's holy, he would have tried.

Zort remained at the cart just long enough to get a rope and a lantern. In a few minutes, he was back at the sewer entrance. Quickly he tied one end of the rope to an iron grating that surrounded the base of a tree, pulling on the rope several times to be certain it was secure. Then he tossed the coil of rope down the sewer and watched it disappear into the blackness.

With the lamp hooked on his belt, the patriarch of the Calabash clan slowly descended into the lightless, evil-smelling world beneath the city streets, praying fervently all the way. Quickly he slipped past the opening of the sewer grating. On three sides of him poured a turbulent waterfall. As he entered the sewer chamber, the falling water echoed and re-echoed with a strange eerie sound. Even with his keen sight, Zort could not see a thing below; the blackness was complete, and it gave him a suffocating feeling, like being buried alive. *If hell is anything like this*, thought Zort, *I rededicate myself to trying to live like a saint.*

Finally he coiled the rope around one leg, reached into a waterproof pouch, took out a match and lit the lantern. The rays of light pierced the black curtain, revealing a grotesque, uninviting world of slime-covered brick and stone walls, flowing water and a seemingly endless tunnel. He took a deep breath and continued down until his feet rested on a ledge that ran along the side of the tunnel. Because of the huge amount of rain flooding the sewer, the raging water was nearly level with the ledge, making it dangerously slippery.

Zort raised the lantern high and shouted as loud as he could. "Krim!"

Back came the echo: *Krim, Krim, Krim, Krim . . .*

Zort held his breath, straining to hear an answer. "Please, God, let him be alive. Take me. I'm old. His family needs him."

Zort walked along the edge for a while, his eyes glued to the raging water. Could anyone possibly survive in that turbulent river? Every so often he shot a quick glance ahead and behind, hoping he would not encounter one of the huge rats that were known to inhabit this subterranean world. What could he do if he met one of those monsters? Zort was not sure that even his vapor balls would have any effect. Suddenly he heard an even stronger sound, the roar of an explosion of water. Then he saw it. Just ahead, the full body of flowing water plunged with a terrible hollow roar into a large pipe plummeting into utter blackness. No one could live in such a fury.

"Oh, my dear Krim; poor, wonderful Krim," cried Zort. "Lord have mercy on his soul." Tears streamed from Zort's eyes, as he realized that however valiantly Krim had tried to survive, at this point his poor body would have been battered into unconsciousness and death.

Dejectedly, Zort dragged himself along the ledge, back to the rope. Climbing up the rope was difficult; it was slippery, and Zort was weary and heartsick. About halfway up, he stopped and looked back. For an instant he remained suspended in the cavernous chamber, the roaring cataract around him. He gave one more glance, a faint hope tucked in the corner of his heart; maybe Krim would call out.

A bright flash of lightning shocked him to reality, and he continued to climb to the street. With the coil of rope around his shoulder, he trudged back to the cart and stood silently, looking at the overturned vehicle in the water, wondering what to do next. The temptation was to merely lie down and die.

But as usual Zort drew upon a great supply of inner strength. "What to do? What do you mean, what to do, Zort W. Calabash?" he murmured to himself. "What you're goin' to do is get that cart home. You'll get into that water and lift the cart to an upright position. Then you'll get it onto the sidewalk and push it home. There will be plenty of time for sorrow. Krim lived a decent, honorable life. For him there's eternal joy. Sorrow is only for the living."

Without hesitation he leaped into the water

and began to tug at the cart in an effort to right the vehicle. Although his body ached, he made a superhuman effort. Slowly the cart was raised. A bit more straining, and it was back on its wheels. Now came the task of getting the cart back onto the sidewalk.

It'll be a miracle if I do it, thought Zort, *but sure I'll give it a try.*

He tied a rope around the cart and climbed up to the sidewalk. Then he threw the rope over an overhanging branch of the fallen tree limb and began to pull, putting his back into it and straining with all his might. Nothing happened.

He took a deep breath and tried again, pulling so hard that his arms seemed to be tearing from his body, his hands almost numb from gripping the rope so tightly. Still he would not give up.

Zort pulled and tugged; he even tried to use his mental powers, but he was so exhausted that there seemed to be no mental energy left. At best he was able to raise the cart only a few inches. He was on the verge of total despair when a pair of hands joined his, and he heard a voice that sounded like an angel.

"Uncle Zort, it'll take both of us to lift the cart."

Zort released his grip, turned and looked into the rain-soaked face of his nephew. For a moment he was stunned. Then, with tears running freely, they embraced, hugging, crying and laughing uncontrollably.

"You're alive. You're alive. Praise be to God," cried Zort.

"I'm alive? I thought you were dead, Uncle." Krim laughed. I was all up and down the street looking for you."

"What happened to you, lad?" asked Zort.

"When the tree branch fell, I was knocked into the water and carried downstream for a while. Then, somehow, I got stuck against the tire of a car and was nearly drowned, but I managed to break loose and come to the surface. I couldn't find a spot to climb up to the sidewalk, so I swam out to the street where the water was shallow and walked back. When I got here to the cart, you were gone. I was sure you'd been carried away by the current, so I started swimming back downstream, looking under all the cars. It took quite a while to search them all. After a while I got to thinking that you had drowned and your body had been carried away. I didn't know what to do. I was heartsick. I kept telling myself it couldn't be true. Somehow Uncle Zort would survive. Then I remembered the tree limb; how it had knocked us into the water. I decided to come back to the cart and search some more around the limb, and there you were, pulling on the rope.

"Well you certainly gave me a scare, young man. I was all set to break the tragic news of your death to Alba and the children."

"Funny" answered Krim, "that's the thing I feared the most to do."

"Okay, enough talk," commanded Zort. "Let's get this cart up on the sidewalk. The temperature is dropping fast. It might change to snow any minute and freeze all this water. So let's move fast."

Krim smiled as he and his uncle, with much effort, raised the cart out of the water. Soon they were rolling the vehicle toward 86th Street. Neither of them spoke. They had a lot to think about. A few minutes later they were at the wide street.

A beveled sidewalk made it easier to roll the cart into the street, and the rain had let up a bit, making it less difficult to cross the flowing water. The two of them looked both ways. No cars or buses were in sight. Though, they suddenly realized, snow was now mixed with the rain, so it was more difficult to see great distances.

"Quick, let's get this thing to the other side," ordered Zort.

Except for a lot of hard work, the rest of the trip to 85th Street was relatively uneventful. With great joy they guided the cart down the ramp of the apartment house courtyard as patches of white were forming from the heavy snow that was now falling. A few minutes later they were inside the basement, soaking wet, half-frozen, exhausted, but none the worse for the wear and tear.

The two little men pushed the cart to the area near the oil tank and sat down for a few minutes.

"You know, Uncle Zort, I really didn't think we'd make it home."

Zort just smiled.

"But I guess I should have learned long ago, when you say we're going to make it, we'll sure enough make it.

Krim looked up at the entrance to the wall space. "I'll bet the family is worried sick about us. We've been gone a long time."

"I think you're right," agreed Zort. Let's leave the cart here and let them know we're safe. We can return for the furniture later."

They climbed the rope ladder to the entrance of the wall space, and from there proceeded up the long ladder that led to the fourteenth floor.

About twenty minutes later, Krim looked up and saw the glow of another lantern. Slowly it got brighter, and he could make out two figures leaning forward looking down the ladder. It was Alba and Starlight.

Soon they were close enough to see the expressions on the women's faces; a mixture of relief, joy and concern. A moment later Krim and Zort were inundated by a profusion of hugging, kissing, laughing and crying.

"Praise the Lord," Grandma repeated over and over.

Alba buried her head in Krim's shoulder, sobbing with joy. "I thought we had lost you. The storm was so terrible. I was so scared, and I didn't know what to do."

"What could possibly have happened to me? I was with Uncle Zort," Krim said hugging Starlight and Buttercup with his other arm while Vand danced up and down with excitement.

The greetings and excitement continued for several minutes. Then in the midst of the excitement, Zort looked around, suddenly realizing that a member of the clan was missing.

"Where's Frollin?"

"Didn't you meet him on the way up?" asked Alba. He went down to the basement, looking for you and Krim."

A tense silence settled on the clan. But just at that moment Frollin walked in. His face was drained of color and seemed near panic.

"What's wrong?" asked Krim.

"A terrible thing is happening in the Di Napoli apartment, and we've got to do something to help them."

"You went into the big people's house?" asked his father, visibly upset. "You've been warned many times never to go there, under any conditions."

"I heard a terrible cry," Frollin answered, as if that would naturally justify his breaking a paramount rule of the clan. "They've got to have our help," he repeated.

"Help them?" interrupted Zort, surprised, even shocked to think that Frollin should make such a preposterous suggestion. "What do you mean, help them? What could be so urgent that they should need our help?"

"A burglar has broken into the apartment and has Mr. and Mrs. Di Napoli and the grandfather tied hand and foot."

"That's not our concern," answered the patriarch with absolute finality. " 'Tis unfortunate, but we cannot interfere, even in the case of burglary."

"You don't understand, Uncle Zort, we've got to help them." The boy paused, his eyes pleading for his uncle to understand. His last words emerged as almost a sob . . . "He's about to murder them."

7 ✳ A Life and Death Decision

Black Jack's face was wearing the sick grin of a madman. His bony fingers curled tightly around the handle of his switchblade as he waved it close to the faces of his victims. For several moments Jack remained silent. No words were necessary.

The tension was too much for Mary Di Napoli. She began to sob, while at the same time desperately trying to contain herself so as not to wake the children.

"For God's sake, take whatever else you want," said John Di Napoli. "We won't expose you. It's all insured, so we'll be repaid."

"So what, big spender, you still gotta report the robbery to collect," snapped Jack.

"But we won't identify you. You'll be safe. Why add murder to it?" answered Mr. Di Napoli.

"Hey! Hey! Cool it Mr. D. I don't trust nobody. No exceptions," Jack said, with a sneer. Then his face returned to a smile. "Besides . . ." he paused, made a waving gesture with his knife and spoke almost casually, ". . . what's another few murders, more or less."

"Look," pleaded Mr. Di Napoli, straining at his ropes and flushed with emotion, "take me as a hostage and let my wife and father-in-law go."

"What am I supposed to do, feed you for the rest of my life. Na, ya all gotta go. Nothing personal, like I said. I just never leave witnesses. It was your tough luck that Pops here stumbled downstairs. He shoulda been asleep."

Black Jack looked at his watch. "Hey! It's getting late. I gotta finish up. He leaned over his victims and spoke in a low, raspy voice. I don't wanna hear any noise from you when I'm inside. Anybody that wakes up and comes down is gonna get it like you." He smiled. "Got it?"

They had not mentioned the children, but

obviously he had done a lot of research and knew exactly who was in the household.

Jack stood up and looked around, playing the beam of his light around the room. It rested on a breakfront, which aroused his curiosity.

"Let's see. What've we got here?" He walked over and opened the glass door, flooding its contents with light. There were dozens of pieces of antique silverware, valuable even to an untrained eye.

"Well, well, well, isn't this a nice little collection." He turned and shot the beam across the room, illuminating the three figures tied against the wall. "Hey, big spender, you shoulda sold tickets to this place. It's a real museum."

Jack returned his attention to the silverware, examining individual items very carefully. "Boy! I almost overlooked all this. I must be slipping. All the dope I learned about this place, and no one ever mentioned this stuff. Ah, they're dummies. All they know is diamonds and cash. They got no class. I'll get a real bundle for this stuff.

"Wait till Jake the Snake see this stuff," Jack mumbled to himself. "His eyes'll bug outta his head. In all his years of fencing, he ain't never seen the likes of this."

He set to work carefully packing the valuable items in his bag. It was a good night's work. Yet somehow he felt that he had overlooked something. Maybe it was the Wedgewood jasper plaques in the living room. They might be worth taking. He picked up his bag and left the dining room.

Strolling casually into the living room, he looked the place over with the assurance and arrogance of a victorious general surveying a conquered land. He stopped at the doorway and slowly inspected the room with his flashlight. To his right was a grand piano, below which Mountain lay in deep slumber.

"I always wanted to play one of these things," mused Jack. "Too bad my old man was always broke."

The flashlight beam scanned to his left and illuminated the large fireplace constructed of beautiful carved Italian marble. *Boy! that's class*, he thought. *A real fireplace in a city apartment.*

The light shot across the room to an ornate stairway leading to a balcony that continued around two sides of the room. Five bedrooms and three bathrooms were located off the balcony. The walls of the living room were paneled in walnut to a level of ten feet. From there to the ceiling they were covered by an elegant brocaded wallpaper. Jack pointed the light straight up. "Wow. That must be a twenty-foot ceiling. They sure don't make'em like that no more."

He turned and walked over to the china

closet in the corner of the living room and opened the glass door. Once again his light beam reflected off the delicate porcelain pieces. On the second shelf there were six Wedgewood jasper plaques.

I'm sure I can get a couple of grand for the set, thought Jack as he wrapped them carefully and put the plaques in his bag.

The storm had subsided, and it was very quiet, so that even the soft rustle of the bag could be heard. He lifted it from the floor. "This is getting pretty heavy. I'd better finish up and get going." Jack turned and headed for the dining room.

❄   ❄   ❄

Zort W. Calabash stood erect, stretching to his full five and a quarter inches, his eyes sparkling and his expression one of inner strength, firmness and, above all, authority. No one spoke for a full minute. Krim, Alba, Grandma and the children waited silently as Zort prepared to address them.

" 'Tis obvious by the looks on your faces you consider the situation in the Di Napoli apartment as being of the utmost gravity."

There were some silent nods of agreement.

"Let me start out by saying that I am not

devoid of emotion, nor am I insensitive to the gravity of the situation. But . . . there is much more involved than just the fate of the Di Napolis. What we must address ourselves to is the fact that what is also involved is the very survival of our entire community.

"Must I remind you that we have managed to survive as a community, in spite of a thousand different kinds of threats to our lives, mainly because we have held steadfastly to our one supreme rule." He held up his long finger and looked around. "One crucial, unbendable rule. Under no circumstances do we ever involve ourselves in the affairs of the big people. Never! No matter how grave the reason."

Zort paced a few steps, deep in thought, thinking over his last statement, then turned to them. "Besides, we cannot be certain that the intruder really intends to murder those people."

No one answered for a few seconds, then Frollin spoke. "I saw his face. There's no question about it. He's going to kill them.

"Nevertheless," replied Zort "we must not let our emotions overcome our intellect and our sense of survival. I repeat, our sense of survival. It is an unfortunate tragedy, but we must think of the community and stand firm—no interference!"

Uncle Zort, some rules have got to be broken

once in a while," said Frollin. "Some rules don't mean the same thing all the time."

Zort walked up to the young man and addressed his words directly to him. "It may sound simple. Break the rule. It can't hurt to do it just once. But this is not just any rule. It is one of our paramount rules. Do you understand what you're saying? Do you have any idea what it would mean if just one of us were ever captured by the big people? It would be a catastrophe for the entire community."

Zort paused, then continued in a softer tone, "Frollin, I know where your heart lies. You are sensitive to the suffering of others. 'Tis a commendable quality. But think. We are barely bigger than the palm of a big person's hand." He placed his old hand gently on the lad's shoulder. "If one of us were captured, it would be the most spectacular scientific find in history for the big people. It would reveal our existence, and they would surely conclude that where there was one, there would be others. There would be a mad rush to find the rest of us. They'd tear out the walls and ceilings and never stop searching night and day. They'd scheme and set all sorts of ingenious traps. We'd be worth a fortune to research or to sideshows in circuses, or to use as toys or pets. For us it would be devastation, heartache, suffering without end. We'd merely be freaks in the big people's world. Being caught would be a fate far worse than death. So you're talking about the death of a few big people as opposed to the living death of our entire community."

Zort stopped and waited for a few seconds.

"But they're going to die," repeated Frollin.

"You speak of death? Zort thundered. "You speak of death as though it were unknown to us." He stepped back a pace and surveyed the entire family. "If death be our unit of measure, let us all reflect on the endless times that death has visited our community. Think of the fifty souls that journeyed to the great castle of Tara. Fifty started, and only seventeen were alive when they reached the castle. Or the dreaded fire of 1835, which leveled seven hundred buildings in New York. Nearly our entire community remained in the walls, not daring to come out, for fear of being caught by the big people. Lord knows, there's no need to remind me that death is a part of life. For us, death has always been a member of the family."

A great hush descended on them. They clung to each other. Grandma cradled Buttercup and Vand in her arms. Starlight stood close to her mother, and Krim's arms lay across Frollin's shoulder. Zort slowly walked away in deep thought.

As the moments passed, the tension increased. Frollin stood next to his father impatiently, fidgeting and following his uncle's movements with his deep brown eyes.

Suddenly he whirled around and spoke to Krim in a subdued, but determined tone. "I'm going down there!" There was a look of desperation on his face. "If no one else is willing, I'll do it myself." He turned to leave.

Krim grabbed his son's arm. "Wait a minute. Don't be a hothead," he said firmly. "Think! Think of what you're saying."

"I am thinking" answered Frollin. "I'm thinking about those poor people down there, about to be murdered."

"Don't you think Uncle Zort understands what's happening? Don't you think he has feelings? Look at him, wrestling with the problem; agonizing, balancing our lives against theirs. He may have said no to you. But it's not his final word. There's a furious battle going on inside of him right now."

"Father, I'm not asking him to go. He's struggling with his conscience. Well, I have a conscience, too. I feel that I couldn't live with myself if I stand here and do nothing."

"You missed his whole point. There's more than you know involved. You can't just think of yourself and your feelings. If you go down there, you'll be shattering the discipline that has kept us alive all these centuries. Look around," Krim continued. "Look at your mother, your brother, your sisters and Grandma. Think of the O'Toole family and all the other families in this building. Are you ready to sacrifice all their lives? 'Cause that's just what you'll be doing if you go down there."

Frollin remained silent.

"Look," added Krim, "if it were you risking your life for what you believed to be right, I'd say go. But the well-meaning miscalculations of one of us could spell total disaster for all. That's why discipline in our ranks is so essential."

He placed his hands on Frollin's shoulders. "Give Uncle Zort a chance. He's working it out. We've got to trust in him. He has never failed to make an unselfish decision. Besides," Krim added, "what he may be doing is trying to figure out what course of action we could take if we were to go down there."

Frollin remained silent, but he stayed where he was.

For a while the scene became a tableau. No one moved lest they distract the patriarch and waste precious time. Finally Grandma walked over to Zort, who was so deep in thought that he was not even aware of her presence.

"Son."

"What is it?" asked Zort almost in a whisper.

"Well . . . I was thinking, for years we've been living off the big people. We live in their houses, eat their food, use their medicines, get information from their books. Sure now, there have been few opportunities for us to return anything to them for these blessings. Would this not be a chance to pay them back for our own lives?"

Zort waited a few seconds, his hand rubbing his long chin. "I hear what you're saying, Mother, But it's so dangerous."

Suddenly Zort felt someone tugging at his pants leg. He looked down. It was Buttercup, her angel-face looking up and her soft white arms extended. "Can I talk to you Great-Uncle Zort?"

"May I talk to you," he corrected.

"May I talk to you?" she repeated.

Zort reached down and picked up Buttercup, snuggling her close to him. "What is it little angel?"

She placed her tiny hand on his face. "Uncle Zort, I'm worried."

"What about?"

"Well . . . I'm worried about what's going to happen downstairs." Tears formed in Buttercups big soft brown eyes. "Uncle Zort, is that bad man going to kill Mountain and the children?"

Zort held her tight and remained silent for several seconds. Then he responded ever so softly. "Mountain and the children will be all right. I promise you. I don't know what we can do. It'll be very difficult. But . . ." He took a breath. "But I suppose we really should try. As I always say, trying is what counts." Zort lowered Buttercup to the floor and straightened up. Krim and Frollin stood there, waiting; not knowing what to expect.

"Well! Why are you standing there like sticks," roared Zort. "Quick, get some ropes! Get the tools! We're going to catch us a burglar."

8 ✳ Attack Black Jack

The thought of interfering in the affairs of the big people was electrifying. Normally those who were allowed to enter the big people's homes were a select few, individuals such as Uncle Zort and Mr. O'Toole, who had spent decades in training. And even their forays were done with the utmost care, to absolutely minimize the possibility of an encounter with the big people.

In seconds, Krim had filled the tool bag with the necessary items, while Frollin had hoisted a huge coil of rope over his shoulder.

After brief instructions from Zort, they followed their uncle down the ladder.

As each step brought them closer to the Di Napoli apartment, Zort wondered again if they were doing the right thing. Here they were, the three men of the house, putting their lives on the line. But when they reached the small door to the apartment, all thoughts of turning back were rejected.

Zort held up the lantern and spoke in a hushed voice. "Are you certain you want to go through with this?"

The other two nodded yes.

"Okay. Remember, speak only when absolutely necessary. Be careful not to make any kind of noise and work as fast as possible."

Zort and Krim removed the two bars from the door and unlatched it. Then, after extinguishing the lamp, the patriarch silently slipped into the apartment, while Krim and Frollin waited in the dark. He returned a few minutes later.

I made a quick survey. The burglar is in the dining room where he has the Di Napolis bound. Believe it or not, Mountain is under the piano fast asleep. We'll have to work fast; the burglar is tying up his bag. Here's what I want you to do."

Zort described his plan of action, and they were ready to go in. "While you two are doing that, I'll round up the animals. They're the key to this whole thing."

They gathered around the door. "Here we go," he said. "May the saints be with us." Zort opened the door a crack. It was quiet. He opened it further and poked his head out. Except for Mountain sleeping under the piano, there was no one in sight.

"Quick!" commanded Zort. "Into action."

Three little figures slipped into the living room and went straight to work.

"You uncoil the rope, and I'll carry it across the room and wind it around the piano leg," instructed Krim.

Meanwhile, Zort had found Hour Hand in the far corner, under the hi-fi cabinet.

"Hello" blinked the turtle. "It's . . . good . . . to . . . see . . . you . . . again."

"The feeling is mutual," said Zort impatiently. "I'm afraid the pace of our conversation will have to quicken. We have an emergency on our hands."

"Yes . . . I . . . know what . . . you . . . mean. There's a stranger . . . in . . . the apartment."

"He's more than just a stranger. He's a burglar and a killer. We'll have to work as a team if we're going to rescue the Di Napolis."

"I'll . . . do . . . anything . . . I can," assured Hour Hand.

Zort explained his plan of action and told Hour Hand what he had to do.

"We'll also need Rhinoceros. Where do you suppose he is?" asked Zort.

"Probably . . . in . . . his . . . favorite place . . . the kitchen."

"That's a problem."

"Why" asked Hour Hand.

"Because we can't go through the dining room. The burglar and the Di Napolis are in there."

"There's another way . . . into the . . . kitchen."

"Where is it?" asked Zort.

"Across . . . the . . . room, . . . near . . . the piano. Do . . . you . . . see . . . the counter?"

"Yes."

"Well . . . there's . . . a . . . serving . . . panel . . . that . . . you . . . can . . . slide . . . open."

"Thank you," interrupted Zort. "Just be ready and listen for the big crash. Remember, stay close by. You're not too fast on your feet," he called out softly as he made his way across the living room.

By now he had totally forgotten the potential danger to himself and his nephews and was completely preoccupied by his concern for the safety of the Di Napolis. Time was running out fast. *Why did I take so long to make up my mind.*

If they're killed, it'll be partially my fault, he thought.

Zort hurried across the room carrying his bag of tools. He sprang onto the counter and investigated the sliding panel, which sat on a well-polished brass track. It was opened just enough to allow Zort to slip in his long, thin fingers.

Placing one foot against the frame, the little man pulled firmly against the panel. A few seconds later the panel was open, and Zort was standing on a counter in the kitchen.

"Now, where is that lazy cat," murmured Zort as he scanned the room. He leaped to the floor, walked to the center of the kitchen and searched beneath the large kitchen table.

Nothing in sight. To the right was the sink, dishwasher, stove and washer and dryer—no place for Rhinoceros to hide. He was obviously not in the kitchen.

A sense of desperation gripped Zort. Rhinoceros was essential if the plan to save the Di Napolis was going to work. He ran to the pantry door, which was slightly open, and stepped inside. The room was pitch black.

"Rhinoceros!" called Zort. "Are you in here?"

All was silent.

"Rhinoceros!" he called louder.

At first there was silence. Then Zort felt a

set of wiry whiskers and a cold wet nose brush against him.

"What are you doing in here, little man?" asked Rhinoceros.

"Looking for you."

"For what" he asked, a bit annoyed for being awakened from a dead sleep.

I need your help," answered Zort.

"What for?"

"The Di Napolis are in terrible trouble. A burglar has broken into the apartment and is going to kill Mr. and Mrs. Di Napoli and Nonno.

"That's terrible. That's awful," said Rhinoceros, suddenly becoming very angry.

"Didn't you hear the burglar?" asked Zort.

"I heard some strange noises. But I was so comfortable in here, I didn't bother to see what it was!"

"You ought to be ashamed of yourself," scolded Zort.

"What do you expect. I'm only a cat. Anyway, what do you want me to do?"

I have a plan. But we'll need help from Bee-flat and Mountain."

"How ya gonna get that crazy bird out of the cage?"

"Let me worry about that. Here's what I want you to do." Zort carefully explained his plan to Rhinoceros. ". . . Do you understand the plan?"

"No problem, he'll be the sorriest burglar that ever lived," answered the cat, as he scampered off to the living room.

Next Zort climbed up to the large bird cage, ducked under the velvet cover and squeezed through the bars. For a moment he stood there looking up at a large parrot who was perched on a wooden bar.

She was a yellow-headed Amazon, with yellow-gold feathers around the head, green body and green wings with blue tips, powerful bill and sharp claws. Her red eyes stared incredulously at Zort, not sure of how to react to the intruder. But she quickly regained her composure and was about to leap upon her uninvited guest.

"Hold it!" commanded Zort, in an authoritative voice.

"I can't believe it! You're speaking my language! Who are you?" asked Beeflat.

"There's no time for introductions" said Zort. "Your masters are about to be killed. Do you want to help them?"

"Anything," said Beeflat. "But how can I help them in this cage?"

Zort quickly opened the cage door and explained his plan of action. Moments later, Beeflat was making her way into the living room.

Now to wake up sleeping beauty, thought Zort. Back through the panel, a few leaps and jumps brought him to the spot where Mountain was sleeping. The big shaggy dog was curled up with his head tucked next to his hind legs, looking like a giant ball of fur with a tail.

Zort walked up to Mountain and pulled on his floppy ear. "Come on, Mountain, wake up! Wake up, you lazy beast!"

The dog didn't stir. Zort pulled harder.

"Wake up! You big dope." The huge fur ball moved a bit, but then simply rolled over on his side, still unconscious.

Zort was at his wits' end. Mountain was to be the main member of the attack force. Without him, they didn't stand a chance. And time was running out.

Meanwhile, Krim and Frollin were finishing their task.

"Do you see why we secured the rope only to the china closet leg and merely wrapped it once around the piano leg?" asked Krim.

Frollin was not sure of the reason.

"Because, after the burglar trips over the rope, since it is not secured to the piano, we will be able to pull it back to us without having to walk across the open doorway."

Frollin nodded, then walked to the dining room door and peeked in.

Across the room, Zort was still desperately trying to wake Mountain. The best he had done was to get the dog to roll on his back and go back to sleep with not a care in the world. He was making another attempt when Krim came running over.

"Uncle Zort, we've got to move fast. There's no time left."

"What's wrong?"

"The burglar is all packed and ready to leave. He's about to kill the Di Napolis."

"Quick," said Zort, "give me a hand. We've got to wake up Mountain." They both tried pushing and poking the dog, with no success.

Suddenly Rhinoceros approached them. "What's the trouble? he asked.

"We can't wake up Mountain, and we're running out of time!"

"Get out of the way. Lemme try," said the cat.

With lightning quick motion, Rhinoceros sprang onto Mountain's chest and bit his nose violently. As though reacting to an electric shock, Mountain rolled over with a whine, spilling the cat onto the floor.

"Ouch! My nose! Who did that," he growled, looking around, surprised to see Rhinoceros, Zort and Krim. "What are you all doing here? What's wrong?"

"Quick! I can't explain," answered Zort. "Mr. and Mrs. Di Napoli are about to be killed by a burglar, the one you allowed to come into the house."

"Oh, I wondered who he was. I was going to

bark at him when he threw me a beautiful piece of meat. I was hungry so I ate it. I figured a few minutes wouldn't hurt anyone. That's all I remember."

"We'll talk about it later. Here's what I want you to do."

❀   ❀   ❀

The sense of terror in the dining room could not have been more intense. Black Jack stood before his victims, the deadly switchblade in his hand, its razor sharp edge sparkling in the beam of the flashlight.

The three victims sat against the wall, securely tied, their faces chalk white with fear, their eyes pleading for mercy. Yet they knew it was no use. Here was a man who long ago had lost the last shred of compassion.

For a moment he said nothing. Then his white teeth bared themselves in an evil smile. "I bet you don't know what I'm trying to figure out," he hissed.

No one spoke.

"Ah! You don't like games. That's too bad. I'll give you the answer. I'm trying to figure out who I should kill first."

He looked at each one intently. "Okay. Who wants to be first?"

"Please . . . mista . . . you killa me. No toucha my daughter. She's a mamma. She has bambini." Nonno sobbed, tears flowing from his eyes.

"Nice speech, Pop." Black Jack hesitated and looked at his watch. "Hey, it's late. I gotta do this fast." He raised his knife. For an instant, there was silence.

Then . . .

Crash!

Black Jack froze. His smile changed to a look of shock, dismay, then anger. He swung around and crouched, his knife hand thrust forward. Thoughts of panic flashed into everyone's mind. Was it one of the children?

Like a raging beast, Black Jack leaped across the room, tore open the dining room door and, without hesitation, ran through the doorway in pursuit of another victim.

Then pandemonium broke loose. The intruder plummeted forward, frantically trying to regain his balance before he crashed to the floor. The knife flew from his hand, and for a moment he was totally disoriented.

With perfect coordination, all members of the attacking team went into action.

Frollin pulled back the rope and wound it into a coil.

Krim raced across the living room floor,

lifted Black Jack's knife and carried it under the china closet. The least they could do was to get rid of the killer's weapon.

Zort leaped onto a small table and toppled the telephone receiver from its hook. In rapid succession, he pushed against the button marked nine, then the button marked one, twice. There was a buzzing sound a click.

"Hello, nine-one-one, can I help you?"

Zort knelt down and yelled into the receiver. "Emergency, emergency. Murder, murder, come quick! 1445 Park Avenue, Apartment Fourteen G."

"I'll connect you with the police. One moment."

Once again a clicking sound then a voice. "Sixty-eight Precinct, Sergeant Muller. What's the problem?"

"Murder, murder! Come quick. Murder, 1445 Park Avenue, Apartment Fourteen G. Hurry!" Zort yelled frantically.

"We're on our way. May I have your name and telephone number, sir?"

"No time, murder, please come quick."

Zort turned from the phone to watch the animals. They had come from all directions. Mountain, Rhinoceros, Beeflat and Hour Hand had pounced on Black Jack as soon as he hit the floor. No single one of them was a match for the vicious killer, but together they were a formidable force.

Growling and snarling, Mountain caught one of Black Jack's arms in his powerful jaws. He bit and tore at the villain, sinking his teeth in the flesh, growling ferociously.

Meanwhile, Beeflat had alighted on Jack and was clawing and pecking at him furiously. While flapping her wings, she dug her razor-sharp claws into the burglar's face, lacerating his skin. No matter how often Jack shook his head, casting off Beeflat, she would simply descend again with greater ferocity.

Rhinoceros, his tail fat as a fox and with claws extended like ten sharp daggers, was attacking Jack's free arm. He would lunge, bite and scratch. The burglars would beat his arm to the floor, sending the cat sprawling across the room. But the cat would not give up his attack.

Hour Hand did his best, which was to clamp his sharp jaws onto one of Black Jack's ears. He held on with a vice grip, not letting go even when Jack pitched his head right and left.

The scene was one of pure chaos: growling, screeching, meowing, fur flying, arms and legs flailing. Black Jack fought furiously. His main adversary was Mountain. If he could rid himself of the dog, he would be back in control.

With this thought in mind, he made a desperate attempt to reach into his back pocket where he kept a spare knife. Once, twice, three times, he reached in, but had to battle off the attacks of Rhinoceros, Beeflat and Hour Hand. Then finally he was successful. His fingers curled around the weapon, and he drew it from his pocket. A quick press of a button, and its deadly blade shot forward.

The commotion had startled Mr. and Mrs. Di Napoli and Nonno. They could not imagine what was happening.

"What is it? What's going on? Can you see, John?"

"I don't know. But I'm going to find out," he answered as he struggled to raise himself. Leaning against the wall and pushing with his feet, Mr. Di Napoli inched his way to a standing position. And then with his ankles tightly bound, he managed to hobble over to the dining room door.

The commotion was still at fever pitch in the other room. John poked his head in and gasped. He couldn't believe his eyes: his household pets were fighting like wild jungle beasts.

But he also saw Jack obtain his second knife. "Oh no! Oh no!" John cried out.

"What is it? What is it?" screamed Mary, nearly hysterical.

John Di Napoli pushed the door open with his shoulders, his eyes glued to Black Jack. The

villian had extended his arm, holding the switchblade about to strike a deadly blow.

Zort Calabash had also watched Black Jack's
action. But to him, it was a giant arm, holding
a huge swordlike weapon. There was no way he
or his nephews could prevent the killer from
striking his blow . . . or was there? A large Chinese
vase sat on top of the china closet. Zort concentrated. The vase rocked. He concentrated harder.
The vase bolted from the shelf and smashed on
the floor, just barely grazing Jack. It did not
knock him unconscious, but the blow was enough
to startle him, causing him to lower his arm. Yet
a moment later, he was prepared to strike again.

John Di Napoli mustered every ounce of
strength and hopped across the room. Black Jack
extended his arm, gripping the knife over Mountain. John made a desperate leap.

Down he came. Both feet landing squarely
on the villain's arm. There was the sickening sound of fracturing bone, and an agonizing
scream from Black Jack.

John lost his balance and fell to the floor.
Then there was a second scream, as Mrs. O'Callighan, the housekeeper, came running out of
her room.

The animals were in a fury. John Di Napoli
lay on the living room floor unable to raise himself, wondering what would happen next.

Black Jack was now wild-eyed with terror. With a convulsive surge of energy, he tore himself loose, bleeding from the face and hands, his right arm hanging limp. He reached down and picked up the switchblade knife with his left hand and stood over Mr. Di Napoli, the weapon raised. He did not even take notice of Mountain and Rhinoceros tearing at his legs.

"This is for you, big spender," he screamed.

Suddenly, the front floor flew open with a loud crash. Two policemen tore into the room, their guns pointed at the killer.

"Drop the knife."

Jack hesitated, considering whether he should kill his victim even at the cost of his own life. But, in the end, he dropped his knife.

"Okay! Okay! Just get these crazy animals off of me," he pleaded.

In quick succession, John and Mary Di Napoli and Nonno were untied as Black Jack was taken away in handcuffs.

The nightmare was over.

❖   ❖   ❖

An hour later, after answering a long series of questions by a police detective, Mr. and Mrs. Di Napoli, Nonno and Mrs. O'Callighan were sitting in the living room having coffee. Miraculously, the children had slept through the entire affair. A great deal of attention was being showered on the animals. Mountain was sitting next to John Di Napoli, his master stroking the dog's large furry head. Rhinoceros was snuggled comfortably on Mrs. D's lap. Hour Hand had settled near the coffee table, while Beeflat was perched on Nonno's shoulder.

It had been a harrowing experience. One that would never be forgotten. Outside, the snow was falling gently, covering trees, cars, streets and sidewalks. Large snowflakes sailed down gracefully, glistening as they passed the streetlights. For several minutes everyone was silent, each one absorbed in a stream of thoughts, but all aware that this Christmas they would have something for which they would be truly grateful.

Mrs. Di Napoli finally broke the silence. She repeated herself for the fifth time.

I still don't understand it. Who called the police? Why did my vase fall to the floor just at that critical moment; and what made the burglar trip?"

"Sure now, it was ghosts. Many times my sainted mother told me of their ways. You know, sometimes they do those kinds of things," suggested Mrs. O'Callighan, her eyes rolling, looking around the room.

"You know . . ." said Mr. Di Napoli in a mystified tone, "if I didn't know better, I'd swear these animals had been led by someone." He paused. "Well . . . anyway, whoever it was, God bless them and give them the merriest of Christmases.

❈   ❈   ❈

The Calabash Clan was gathered in the family area of their living quarters with its multicolored drapes covering the drab walls. Grandma was in her rocker, holding Buttercup. The others were seated on chairs and low stools. Everyone was feeling a great sense of pride and contentment. They had accomplished what had seemed impossible. During the season of giving, they had given the big people the greatest of all gifts, life. Zort, who had changed back to his usual formal attire, stood in the middle of the room. For a few moments he surveyed the group. Then he spoke.

"Tonight I am a proud man. No one could have a more loving and courageous family. You are all to be commended."

"Uncle Zort, I think you deserve the lion's share of the credit. We only did what you told us to do," said Krim.

"That may be so, but I had to be goaded to action."

At that Zort walked over to Frollin, who was sitting on a stool in the corner. "I have a special thanks for Frollin. He doesn't speak much, but when he does, he usually makes a great deal of sense. There is a family down there who owe their lives to Frollin's good heart and determination. And just as important, he has reminded us that if we want to remain part of the human family, we must be willing to risk our own lives if others really need our help."

"Besides," called out Buttercup, "now we know that as little as we are, we can help the big people."

Everyone laughed, and Zort said, "Well, there's still a lot of work to be done. Christmas is only two weeks away. We'll make ourselves a beautiful tree, courtesy of the Di Napolis. There's food to be gathered, presents to be made and fun to be had. He paused, then smiled. It will be a real challenge, living above the Di Napoli apartment. But with such a great clan, we're going to be just fine."

Everyone fully agreed with Uncle Zort.

It turned out to be one of the most wonderful Christmases the Calabash Clan could remember. Zort and Krim took them up to the roof in the early morning hours to play in the undisturbed snow. Krim made beautiful toys for Van and Buttercup. Alba and Starlight knitted colorful sweaters for the men. Zort took a small branch from the Di Napolis' tree, and they decorated it with their beautiful balls. The great joy of the season lasted long into the New Year, and eventually, their home was complete with colorful walls and pretty furniture. But most of all, the new home of the Calabash Clan was made beautiful by the wonderful, loving little people who inhabited the dwelling.

THE END